A GREEK ESCAPE

A GREEK ESCAPE

BY

ELIZABETH POWER

First published in Great Britain 2013
by Mills & Boon, an imprint of Harlequin (UK) Limited.
Large Print edition 2013
Harlequin (UK) Limited, Eton House,
18-24 Paradise Road, Richmond, Surrey TW

LP

© Elizabeth Power 2013

ISBN: 978 0 263 23228 8

Harlequin (UK) policy is to use papers that are natural,
renewable and recyclable products and made from
wood grown in sustainable forests. The logging and
manufacturing process conform to the legal environmental
regulations of the country of origin.

Printed and bound in Great Britain
by CPI Antony Rowe, Chippenham, Wiltshire

For Alan—and all those
wonderful sandwiches that kept me going!

CHAPTER ONE

'THAT'S IT! THAT'S the one we want! Stop wasting time, you idiot, and take it!' The camera clicked the second before the bird took off from its rock and flapped away over the crystalline water. 'Didn't think I'd let you get away, did you?'

From her vantage point on the rocky hillside overlooking the shingle beach Kayla Young swung round with a swish of long blonde hair, embarrassed that someone might have overheard her. There was nothing but a warm wind, however, passing over the craggy scrubland, and the relentless sun beating down from a vividly azure sky, and Kayla's shoulders drooped in relief.

She wasn't sure when she had first started talking to herself. Perhaps coming away all by herself to this lovely island wasn't doing much for her sanity, she thought, grimacing. Or perhaps it was a defence mechanism against the knowledge that today, back in England, the man she had thought she'd be spending her life with was an hour away from marrying someone else.

The wounds of betrayal were no longer so raw but the scars remained, and in defiance of them Kayla brought the SLR's viewfinder to eye level again. Only her clamped jaw revealed the tension in her as, silently now, she appraised the beauty around her.

Misty blue mountains. Translucently clear water. Surprisingly hunky Greek…

She'd been following a line inland, coming across the deserted beach, but now Kayla brought her viewfinder back to the shoreline in a swift doubletake.

Bringing her camera down, she could see him clearly without the aid of the zoom lens, and she found herself homing in on him with her naked eyes.

Black wavy hair—which would have been way past his collar had he been wearing one—fell wildly against the hard bronze of his neck. In a black T-shirt and pale blue jeans he was pulling fishing tackle from the wooden boat he had recently beached, and from the contoured muscles of his arms, and the way the dark cotton strained across his wide muscular chest, Kayla instantly marked him as a man who worked with his hands. A battered old truck was parked close to her rock, on the road just above the beach, and as the man started walking towards it—towards *her*—Kayla couldn't take her eyes off him.

For some reason she couldn't quite fathom she lifted her camera to zoom in on him again, and felt an absurd and reckless excitement in her secret survey. A few days' growth of stubble gave a striking cast to an already strong jaw, mirroring the strength in his rugged features. They were the features of a man toughened by life—a man who looked as fit as he was hard. A man not much more than thirty, who would probably demand his own way and get it—because there was determination in that face, Kayla recognised, as well as pride and arrogance in the way he carried himself, in the straight, purposeful stride of those long legs.

A man one definitely wouldn't want to mess with, she decided, with a curious little tingle down her spine.

She could see it all in every solid inch of him—in the curve of his tanned forehead and those thick winged brows that were drawing together now in a scowl because…

Dear heaven! he was looking up! He had seen her! Seen her pointing the camera straight at him!

As her agitated finger accidentally clicked the shutter closed she realised the camera had caught him—and, as he shouted something out, she realised that he was aware of it too.

She stood stock-still for a second as he quickened his stride; saw him moving determinedly in her direction.

Oh, my goodness! Suddenly she was pivoting away with the stark realisation that he was giving chase.

Why she was running, Kayla didn't know. Surely, she thought, it would have been better to stand her ground and brazen it out? Except that she hadn't felt like brazening anything out with a man who looked so angry. And anyway, what could she have said? *You caught my eye as I was sizing up the view and I couldn't stop looking at you.*

That would really have been asking for trouble, she assured herself, with her blood pounding in her ears and her legs feeling heavy. She darted an anxious glance back over her shoulder and saw the man was gaining on her now, along the stony uphill path that led to the safety of the villa.

And why had she been looking at him anyway?

she reprimanded herself. She had had enough of men to last her a lifetime! It could only have been because he had an interesting face; that was all. Apart from that she wouldn't have looked twice at him if he had rowed across that water accompanied by a fanfare. She had learned the hard way that men were just lying, cheating opportunists—

'Oooh!'

Tripping over a stone, she struggled to keep herself upright, hearing her pursuer's footsteps bearing down on her.

Too late, though. She came a cropper on the hard and dusty path and lay there for a few moments, winded and despairing, but surprisingly unharmed.

She heard the pound of his footsteps and suddenly he was there, standing above her. He was breathing hard, and his tone was rough as he tossed some words at her in his own language.

Utterly awestruck by the speed at which he must have run to have caught up with her, Kayla raised herself up on her elbows, her hair falling like pale rivers of silk over her shoulders.

Having little more than a few words of Greek to get by with, she quavered, 'I don't understand you.' Like him, she was breathless, and shaken by his anger as much as her fall.

He said something else that she couldn't comprehend, while a firm hand on her shoulder—bare save for the white strap of her sun top—pulled her round to face him.

Up close, his features were even more arresting than she'd first imagined. His cheekbones were high and well-defined under dark olive skin. Thick ebony lashes framed eyes that were as black as jet, and his brooding mouth was wide and firm.

'Are you hurt?' His question, delivered roughly in English this time, surprised her, as did that small element of concern.

'No. No thanks to you,' she accused, sitting upright and brushing dust off her shorts, trying to appear less intimidated than she was feeling.

'Then I will ask you again. What do you think you were doing?'

'I was taking photographs.'

'Of me?'

Kayla swallowed, fixing him with wary blue eyes. 'No, of a bird. I snapped you by accident.'

'Accident?' From the way one very masculine eyebrow lifted it was clear that he didn't believe her. His hostile gaze raked over her the pale oval of her face. 'What is this...*accident?*' he emphasised pointedly.

His anger hadn't cooled. Kayla could feel it bubbling just beneath the surface. Despite that, though, his voice had a deep, rich resonance, and although his English was heavily accented his command of her language was obvious as he demanded, 'Exactly how many did you take?'

'Only the one,' she admitted, her breathing still laboured from that chase up the hillside. 'I told you. It was an accident.'

'Well, as far as I'm concerned, young woman, it was one accident too many. Exactly who are you? And what are you doing here?'

'Nothing. I mean, I'm on holiday—that's all.'

'And does the normal course of your holiday usually include sticking your nose into other people's business? Spying on people?'

'I wasn't *spying* on you!' From the way those accusing ebony eyes were studying her, and from the suspicion in his voice, Kayla began to experience real fear. Perhaps he was on the run! Wanted by the police! That would go some way to explaining his anger over being photographed. 'My camera...?' Trying to hide her misgivings, she glanced anxiously around and spotted the expensive piece of equipment lying in the scrub nearby.

Stretching out in a bid to reach it, she was dismayed when the man leaped forward, snatching it up before she could.

'Don't damage it!'

He looked angry enough, she thought. But her camera was something she treasured. A gift to herself to replace her old one after she had discovered Craig was having an affair. Some women comfortate. She went out with her camera and snapped anything and everything as a form of therapy, and over the past three months she had needed all the therapy she could get!

'Give me one good reason why I shouldn't?'

Because it was expensive! she wanted to fling back. And because it's got every photograph I've taken since I got here yesterday. But that would probably only make him more inclined to wreck it, if his mood was anything to go by.

'Perhaps I should simply keep it,' he contemplated aloud, his gaze sweeping over her still pale shoulders and modest breasts with unashamed insolence.

'If it makes you happy,' she snapped, needled by the way he was looking at her. But there was something about that gaze moving over her exposed flesh that produced a rush of heat along with a cautioning tingle through her blood. After all, she didn't have a clue who he was, did she? Supposing he really was wanted by the police?

A bird swooped low out of the pine forest above them, its frenzied shriek making her jump before it screeched away, protesting at the human intrusion.

For the first time Kayla realised just how isolated the hillside was. Apart from a cluster of whitewashed fishermen's houses, huddled above the beach at the foot of the mountain road, there was no other sign of human habitation, while the nearest village with its shop and taverna was nearly three miles away.

As she was scrambling to her feet a masculine arm shot out to assist her.

The sudden act of gallantry was so unexpected after all his hostility that Kayla automatically took the hand he was offering. It felt strong and slightly callused as he pulled her upright, bringing her close to his dominating masculinity. Disconcertingly close.

Her senses awakened to the outdoor freshness of him, to the aura of pulsing energy that seemed to surround him, and to an underlying masculine scent that was all his own.

Swallowing and bringing her head up—in her flat-heeled pumps, she still only reached his shoulder—she took a step back and said in a voice that cracked with an unwelcome tug of unmistakable chemistry, 'I'm not afraid of you.'

'Good.' His tone was terse, and still decidedly unfriendly. 'In that case you won't mind me telling you that I don't like interfering young women depriving me of my privacy. So if you want to enjoy your so-called "holiday",' he emphasised scornfully, dumping the offending camera into her startled hands, 'you'll stay out of my way! Is that clear?'

'Perfectly! And I can assure you, Mr... Mr... No-name,' she went on when he didn't have the decency to tell her. 'I've certainly got no wish to deprive you of anything. Least of all your privacy!' Deciding now that he was probably nothing more dangerous than a bad-tempered local, she pressed on, 'In fact you have my solemn promise that I'll do everything I can while I'm here to see that you maintain it.'

'Thank you!'

Kayla bit back indignation as he swung unceremoniously away, striding back down the path without so much as a glance back.

A few minutes later, coming up through the scrub below the modern white villa where she was staying, she heard the distant sound of a vehicle starting up, and guessed from the roughness of its engine that it was the truck she had seen parked at the head of the beach.

Kayla was still smarting from the encounter as she fixed herself a microwave meal that evening in the villa's well-equipped kitchen. With open-plan floors, exposed roof rafters above its galleried landing and spectacular views over the rolling countryside, the villa belonged to her friends, Lorna and Josh. Knowing how much she needed a break, they had offered Kayla the chance to get away for a couple of weeks.

She had barely met a soul since the taxi driver had dropped her off here yesterday, so why did the first person she bumped into have to be so downright rude?

Slipping the dish into the microwave oven, she stabbed out the settings on the control panel, her agitated movements reflecting her mood.

Still, better that he was rude than charming and

lying through his teeth, she thought bitterly, her thoughts straying to Craig Lymington.

How easily she had fallen for his empty promises. She had believed and trusted him when he'd professed to want to be with her for life.

'He'll break your heart. You mark my words,' her mother had advised unkindly when Kayla had enthused over how the most up-and-coming executive at her company, Cartwright Consolidated, had asked her to marry him.

They had been engaged for two months, and Kayla had been deliriously happy, until that night when she'd discovered those messages on his cell phone and realised that she wasn't the only woman to whom he'd whispered such hollow and meaningless words…

'All men are the same, and the high-flying company type are the worst of the lot!' her mother had warned her often enough.

But Kayla hadn't listened. She'd believed her mother was simply embittered and scarred by her own unfortunate experience. After all, hadn't her own husband—Kayla's father—been a company executive? And hadn't he deserted her in exactly the same fashion fifteen years ago, when Kayla had been just eight years old?

Because of that and her mother's warnings she had grown up determined that the man she eventually decided to settle down with would never treat her in such an abominable way.

But he had, Kayla thought. And she had been rudely awakened and forced to admit—to herself at least—that her mother was right. They *were* the worst of the lot! It was a realisation doubly enforced when she had had to suffer the demeaning overtures of one or two other male members of management who had tried to capitalise on her broken engagement.

After leaving the company where she'd worked with Craig, trying to put the pain and humiliation of what he had done behind her, she might have been able to pick up the pieces of her life if she had been allowed to. But her mother's condescending and self-satisfied attitude—particularly when she'd heard that Craig really was getting married—had made everything far, far worse.

Consequently when Lorna had offered her the chance of escaping to her isolated Grecian retreat for a couple of weeks Kayla had jumped at the chance. It had seemed like the answer to a prayer. A place to start rebuilding her sense of self-worth.

But now, as she took her supper from the bleeping microwave and prodded the rather unpalatable-looking lasagne with a fork, it wasn't thoughts of Craig Lymington that troubled her and upset her determined attempts to restore her equilibrium. It was the face of that churlish stranger she'd been unfortunate enough to cross this morning, and her shocking awareness of him when he'd pulled her to her feet and she'd felt the impact of his disturbing proximity.

Leonidas Vassalio was fixing a loose shutter on one of the ground-floor windows, his features as hard as the stones that made up the ancient farm-house and as darkly intense as the gathering clouds that were closing in over the mountains, warning of an impending storm.

The house would fall down if he didn't take some urgent steps to get it repaired, he realised, glancing up at the sad state of its terracotta roof and the peeling green paint around its doors and windows. The muscles in his powerful arms flexed as he twisted a screw in place.

It was hard to imagine that this place had once been his home. This modest, isolated farmhouse, reached only by a zig-zagging dirt road. Yet this island, with its rocky coast, its azure waters and barren mountains, was as familiar to him as his own being, and a far cry from the world he inhabited now.

The rain had started to fall. Cold, heavy drops that splashed his face and neck as he worked and reflected on the whole complicated mess his life had become.

To the outsider his privileged lifestyle was one to be envied, but personally he was tired of sycophants, superficial women and the intrusion of the paparazzi. Like that interfering slip of a girl he'd caught photographing him on the beach this morning, he thought grimly, ready to bet money that she was one of them. For what other reason would she have been there if she wasn't from some newspaper? He had had enough of reporters to last him a lifetime, and they had been particularly savaging of late.

He had always shunned publicity. Always managed to keep a low media profile. Anyone outside of Greece might not instantly have recognised him, even though they would most certainly have recognised the Vassalio name. It was his brief involvement with Esmeralda Leigh that had thrust him so starkly into the public eye recently.

Nor had it helped when a couple of the high-ranking executives he had trusted to run one of his UK subsidiaries, along with an unscrupulous lawyer, had reneged on a verbal promise over a development deal and given the Vassalio Group bad press—which in turn had brought his own ethics into question. After all, as chairman, Leonidas thought introspectively, the buck stopped with him. But he had been too tied up at the time to be aware of what was going on.

That ordinary people had been lied to and were having their homes bulldozed from under them didn't sit comfortably on his conscience. Nor did being accused of riding roughshod over people without giving a thought to their needs, breaking up communities so as to profit from multi-million-pound sports arenas and retail/leisure complexes and expand on Vassalio's ever-increasing assets. The fact that everyone affected had been compensated—and very well—had been consigned only to the back pages of the tabloids.

He had needed to get away. To forget Leonidas Vassalio, billionaire and successful businessman, for a while and sort out what was important to him. And to do that he had needed to get back to his roots. To enjoy the bliss of virtual anonymity that coming here would offer him. Because only one other person knew he was here. But now it looked as though even that might have been too much to expect, if that nosy little blonde he'd caught snooping around today had lied about why she was here.

And if she hadn't, and she really had been photographing birds, why had she been standing there taking a picture of him? Had she just fancied snapping a bit of local colour? One of the peasants going about his daily business? Or could it be that she'd just happened to like the look of him? he thought, with his mouth twisting cynically. In other circumstances he would have admitted unreservedly to himself that he hadn't exactly been put off by the look of *her*. Especially when he'd noted that she'd been wearing no ring.

But bedding nubile young women wasn't on his agenda right now. Heaven only knew the physical attributes he'd been endowed with acted like a magnet on the opposite sex, and he'd never met one yet that he'd wanted to bed who hadn't been willing, but, no, he determined as he oiled a hinge. Whatever her motives were, and no matter how affected she'd been by that spark of something that had leaped between them and made her pull back from him as though she'd been scorched when he'd pulled her to her feet, that girl certainly hadn't had bedroom games in mind.

She had to be staying in one of those modern villas that had sprung up further down the hillside. That was the direction she had been heading in when he'd caught up with her. He wondered if there was anyone with her, or if she was staying there alone. If she was, he deliberated with his hackles rising, then she had to be here for a reason. And if that reason was to intrude on his peace and solitude…

Finishing what he was doing, annoyed at how much thought he was giving to her, he rushed inside, out of the rain.

She was going to find out the hard way that she couldn't mess with *him!*

CHAPTER TWO

THE THREE-MILE drive to the main village to get provisions had seemed like an easy enough mission, particularly when last night's storm had caused a power cut and made her fridge stop working.

Unless the thing had broken before then, Kayla thought exasperated, having come downstairs this morning to a cabinet of decidedly warm and smelly food.

But the polished voice of the car's satellite navigation system had let her down badly when it had guided her along this track. And now, having parked the car in order to consult the map and try and work out where she was, the little hatchback that her friends kept here for whenever they visited the island refused to start.

She tried again, her teeth clenched with tension.

'Come on,' she appealed desperately to the engine. 'Please.'

It was no good, she realised, slumping back on her seat. It had well and truly packed up.

Lorna had given her the name of someone she could call in an emergency who spoke relatively good English, Kayla remembered, fishing in the glove compartment for the man's number. But when she took her cell phone out of her bag she discovered that she didn't have a signal.

Despairingly tossing the phone onto the passenger seat, she looked around at a Grecian panorama of sea and mountains and, closer to hand, pine woods and stony slopes leading down to this track.

Beyond the open windows of the car the chirruping of crickets in the scrub and the lonely tugging of the wind only seemed to emphasise her isolation. She didn't have a clue where she was.

Glancing back over her shoulder, she recognised way below the group of rocks that ran seaward from the beach where she had seen that surly local yesterday, and that smaller island in the distance, clear as a bell today beneath the canopy of a rainwashed vividly azure sky.

With the sun beating relentlessly down upon her, with an unusable phone and only a broken-down car for company, Kayla glanced wistfully towards what looked like a deserted farmhouse, with a roof that had seen better days peeping above the trees at the end of the track.

Fat chance she had of making a call from there! Or did she?

Sticking her head out of the window and inhaling deeply, she caught the distinct smell of woodsmoke drifting towards her on the scented air.

With her spirits soaring, she leaped out of the car, grabbed her precious camera and set off at a pace, her zipped-back sandals kicking up dust along the sun-baked track.

It was the truck she recognised as she came, breathless, into a paved area at the front of the house. A familiar yellow truck that had her stopping in her tracks even before she recognised its owner.

Wild black hair. Wild eyes. Wild expression.

Oh, no!

Coming from around the side of the house, the surly Greek was looking as annoyed as he looked untamed.

And justifiably so, Kayla decided, swallowing. She had invaded his territory again—unintentionally though it was—and she would have run like the wind if she had realised it a second sooner. As it was, she was riveted to the spot by the sheer dynamism of the man.

In blue denim cut-offs and nothing else but a

dark tan leather waistcoat, exposing his chest and muscular arms, he exuded strength and raw, virile masculinity.

'I thought I told you to stay away from me,' he called out angrily to her, his long, purposeful strides closing the distance between them. 'What do you want?' As if he didn't know! Leonidas thought, his scowling gaze dropping to the camera clutched tightly against her ribcage. 'Didn't you get enough photographs yesterday?'

He looked bigger and distinctly more threatening than he had the previous day, Kayla decided, unnerved. If that were possible!

'I…I just want to use your phone,' she informed him, ignoring his accusation and annoyed with herself for sounding so defensive, for allowing him to intimidate her in such a way.

'My phone?'

She could feel her body tingling beneath the penetrative heat of his gaze. Her T-shirt and shorts felt much too inadequate beside such potent masculinity.

'You *do* have one?' she asked pointedly, trying not to let his unfriendliness get to her. From the way he'd queried her request she might have been asking him to give her a mortgage on Crete! 'My car...' She hated having to tell him as she sent a glance back over her shoulder. 'It's broken down.'

He peered in the direction she'd indicated. But of course he couldn't see it, she realised, because it was way down the track, hidden by trees and scrub. And all she could focus on right then was the undulating muscles of his smooth and powerful chest, which was glistening bronze—slick with sweat.

'Really? And what seems to be the trouble?' he enquired with the sceptical lifting of an eyebrow. He looked at her with such disturbing intensity that Kayla felt as if her strength was being sapped right out of her.

Beneath the thick sweep of his lashes his eyes were amazingly dark, she noticed reluctantly. His nose was proud, his cheekbones high and hard, his mouth firm and well-defined above the dark, virile shadow around his jaw. As for his body...

She wanted to look at him and keep looking at him. *All* of him, she realised, shocked. She was even more shocked to realise that she had never been so aware of a man's sensuality before. Not even Craig's. But he had asked her a question, and all she was doing was standing here wondering how spectacular he would look naked.

Trying to keep her eyes off that very masculine chest, she uttered with deliberate vagueness, 'It won't go.'

That glorious chest lifted as he inhaled deeply. 'Won't move or won't start?' he demanded to know.

Entertaining a half-crazed desire to needle him, Kayla answered with mock innocence, 'It's the same thing, isn't it?'

Now, as those glinting dark eyes pierced the rebellious depths of hers, she realised that this man would know when he was being taken for a fool, and warned herself against the inadvisability of antagonising him.

'Does the engine fire when you turn the ignition key?' he asked, his sweat-slicked chest lifting again with rising impatience.

'No. Nothing happens at all,' she told him, frankly this time. 'So if you could just let me use your phone—if you have a signal—or if you don't...if you have a landline...' A dubious glance up at the house had her wondering if it had fallen into the state it was in long before telephones had been invented.

'It's Sunday,' he reminded her succinctly. 'Who are you going to call?'

She shrugged. 'The nearest garage?' she suggested flippantly, hoping the man whose name she had been given for emergencies would be at home. In fact Lorna had said to call *her* if she needed any help or advice, and right now Kayla felt she'd get more help from her friend back in England than the capable-looking hunk standing just a metre away.

Suddenly, without another word, he was walking past her.

'Show me,' he said over his leather-clad shoulder, much to her surprise.

She virtually had to run to keep up with him.

When they reached the car he held out a hand for the key and Kayla dropped it onto his tanned palm, noticing the cool economy with which he moved as he opened the driver's door and leaned inside to start the ignition.

It fired first time.

'I don't understand...' She turned from the traitorous little vehicle to face the man who had now straightened and was standing there looking tall and imposing and so self-satisfied that she could have kicked him—or the car. Or both! 'I tried and tried,' she stressed, with all the conviction she could muster, because scepticism was stamped on every plane and angle of his hard, handsome face.

He reached into the car again, switched off the

engine and, dangling the key in front of her, said in his heavily accented voice, 'Perhaps you would care to try again?'

She jumped into the car, keeping her defiant gaze level with his, almost willing the little hatchback to refuse to start for her. Because how on earth was he going to believe her if it did?

It did.

She flopped back against the headrest, her eyes closing with a mixture of relief and rising frustration.

'There, you see. It's simple when you know how.'

There was no mistaking the cool derision that drifted down to her through the open door, and suddenly Kayla's control snapped.

'It wouldn't start! I couldn't make it! And if you think I made it all up for some warped reason, just to come here and annoy you, then, believe me, I've got far more important things to do with my time! My phone won't work! My sat-nav's up the creek! And Lorna's fridge has broken down and ruined all the food I bought. And all you can do is stand there and accuse me of lying! Well, I can assure you, Mr... Mr...'

'Leon.'

She looked up at him askance, her blue eyes glistening with angry tears. 'What?'

'My name is Leon,' he repeated. 'And who is this Lorna you mention? Your travelling companion?'

'No. I'm here on my own,' Kayla blurted out without even thinking. A totally frustrating morning had finally taken its toll. 'Lorna owns the villa where I'm staying.' Lorna who—with her husband Josh—had miraculously come to her rescue by offering her a post in their interior design company after Kayla had found it too distressing to stay on at her old job.

'And you say the fridge has broken down?'

'Big-time!' What was he going to do? Drive down and check that she wasn't lying about that as well?

'Have you eaten?'

'What?'

His hand came to rest on the roof of the car as he stooped to address her through the open door. 'I know I'm Greek and you're English, but you seem to be having great difficulty in understanding me. I said, have you eaten?'

'No.'

'Then drive up to the house,' he instructed. 'I'll be along directly.'

What? Kayla nearly said it again, only just stopping herself in time.

He was offering her hospitality? Surely not, she thought, amazed. He was hard, unfriendly, and a perfect stranger to boot.

Well, not perfect, she decided grudgingly. Only in appearance, she found herself silently admitting. Whatever else he was, he was lethally attractive. But some masochistic and warped urge to know more about him—along with the thought of all that festering food she was going to have to throw away—motivated her, against her better judgement, into doing what he had suggested.

He had almost reached the paved yard by the time Kayla put her camera in the boot, out of the sun, having decided it was for the best since it seemed to offend him so much. Involuntarily, her gaze was drawn to his approach.

Unconsciously her eyes savoured the whole sensational length and breadth of him, from those wide shoulders and muscular arms to that glistening bronze chest and tightly muscled waist, right down to his narrow denim-clad hips. Very masculine legs ended in a pair of leather sandals, dusty from his trek along the track.

There was a humourless curl to his mouth, she

noticed as he drew nearer, as though he were fully aware of her reluctant interest in him.

'Around the back,' he advised with a toss of his chin, and waited for her to go ahead of him.

That small act of courtesy seemed oddly at variance with his manners on the whole, she decided, preceding him around the side of the rambling old farmhouse.

Don't talk to any strange men. Never take sweets from a stranger.

Wondering what she was doing, ignoring all those clichéd warnings, Kayla realised her mother would have a fit if she could see her now.

'So…are you going to tell me something about yourself?' Leon whoever-he-was enquired deeply from just behind her.

'Like what?' she responded, still walking on ahead.

'Your name would be a good start,' he suggested incisively.

They had come around to the rear of the house, where weed-strewn shady terraces gave onto an equally overgrown garden.

'It's Kayla,' she told him, following his example and deciding that last names were superfluous.

'Kayla?'

Despite his overall unfriendliness, the way he repeated her name was like the warm Ionian wind that blew up from the sea, rippling through the tufted grass on the arid hills. An unexpected little sensation quivered through her. Or was it the sun that seemed to be burning her cheeks? The warm breeze that was lifting the almost imperceptibly fine hairs on her arms?

'Come.' He gestured to a rustic bench under a canopy of vines. Nearby were some smouldering logs within a purpose-built circle of bricks. Resting on a stone beside it was a grid containing several small plump, freshly prepared fish, their scales gleaming silver in the late morning sun.

'Did you catch those yourself?' She'd noticed a rod and fishing tackle in the back of his truck, and wondered if he went out every day to fish from the boat she'd seen him unloading the previous day.

'Yes, about an hour ago.' He was squatting down, repositioning a log on the fire. 'What's wrong?' he enquired, looking up at her when she still stood there, saying nothing. 'Are you vegetarian?'

She had been silently marvelling at how only this morning those fish had been in the sea—how he had already been down there, brought them back and prepared them for his lunch—but there was no way she was going to tell him that.

'No,' she replied, watching him place the grid on the bricks over the glimmering logs.

'Then sit down,' he commanded, before he turned and strode back into the house.

Left alone, Kayla took a few moments to study its sadly neglected exterior. With its ramshackle appearance, and the odd wild creeper growing out of its walls, it seemed almost to have become part of the hillside that rose steeply above it on one side. She wondered if it might just be a place he had found where it was convenient for him to shack up, and then looked quickly away as he emerged from inside with plates and cutlery and several different kinds of bread in a hand-painted bowl.

'Do I take it that you don't want any?' he called out, noticing that she was still standing where he had left her.

The fish were starting to cook, skins bubbling, their aroma drifting up to her with the woodsmoke, tantalising and sweet.

'No,' she refuted quickly, sitting down on the bench, and earned herself the twitch of a smile from that mocking, masculine mouth as he set the plates and cutlery down on a small, intricately wrought iron table that looked as though it had seen every winter for decades. 'So, why are you asking me to lunch if you want to be left alone?'

'Good question,' he responded without looking at her. He was using a fish slice to turn their lunch. Spitting oil splashed onto the glowing logs, making them sizzle. 'Perhaps it's the best way of keeping an eye on you,' he said when he had finished.

'Why?' She fixed him directly with eyes that were as vivid as cornflowers. 'Why are you so worried about my bothering you? Why do you think I need keeping an eye on?' she queried, frowning. 'Unless...'

'Unless what?' he urged, calmly setting the fish slice aside.

Her heart was beating unusually fast. 'You have something to hide.'

Squatting there, with his hands splayed on his bunched and powerful thighs, he was studying her face with such unsettling intensity that for a few moments Kayla wondered if her original supposition about him was right. He really was on the run from the law. Why else would he object so strongly to being photographed?

Leonidas made a half-amused sound down his nostrils. 'Don't we all?' he suggested through the charm of a feigned smile, and thought, *Particularly you, my scandal-mongering little kitten.*

For a moment he saw tension mark the flawless oval of her face. What was it? he wondered. Excitement? Anticipation? The thrill of getting some juicy snippet about him to pad out some gossip column she couldn't fill with the misfortunes of some other unsuspecting fool?

'Does valuing my personal space necessarily mean I have to be hiding something?' he put to her, a little more roughly, and saw her mouth pull down as she contemplated his question.

It didn't. Of course it didn't, Kayla thought in an attempt to allay her suspicions about him.

'No,' she responded, pushing her hair back behind one ear, wondering why she was finding it so easy to let herself be persuaded.

Disconcertingly, those midnight-black eyes followed her agitated movement before he swung away from the fire, went back into the house.

'What about you?' he quizzed, after he'd returned with a couple of chunky glasses, which he also set down on the table before returning to the makeshift barbecue.

'What *about* me?' Kayla enquired, noticing how the muscles bunched in his powerful legs as he dropped down on his haunches. Her mouth felt unusually dry.

'You're here on your own,' he remarked. 'Which can mean only one of two things.'

'Which are?' she prompted cautiously, watching him wield the fish slice and slide some fish onto one of the earthenware plates he had brought from the house. He handed it to her, before dishing out another portion for himself.

'You're either running away...' He put his own plate down on an upturned fruit crate opposite the bench and retrieved the rustic bowl from the table.

'Or...?' she pressed, swallowing, feeling his eyes watching her far too intently as she took a chunk of the wholesome-looking bread he was offering her.

'Or...you're chasing something.'

'Like what?' she invited, frowning, feeling as though those keen dark eyes were suddenly giving her a mental frisking. She had the feeling that behind that casual manner of his lurked a blade-sharp brain that was assessing her every reaction, and that every word and response from her was being systematically weighed and measured.

Leonidas's mouth compressed. 'Dreams. A good time.' He moved a shoulder in a deceptively non-chalant way. *Another sensation-charged story to smear the Vassalio name.* 'So which is it for you, lovely Kayla?'

With her pulse doing an unexpected leap at the way he had addressed her, Kayla viewed him with mascara-touched lashes half-shielding her eyes.

How could he be so perceptive? So shrewd? He was living here like a gypsy. Whether he was alone or with someone she couldn't tell—although from what he had said she would have put money on it that there wasn't anyone else in residence. A man close to nature, who wasn't afraid of hard work, yet with a keen mind behind all that physical strength and potent energy. And a comprehension of human nature that even Craig with his university degree and his boardroom ambitions hadn't possessed.

She had no intention, however, of telling this unsettling hunk that his first assumption was right. That she *was* running away, and that she hadn't fully realised it until now. Her broken engagement and her recently bruised heart weren't things she wanted to discuss with anyone—least of all a man she had only just met, who didn't really want her there…even if he obviously felt obliged to share his lunch with her.

Looking down at her plate, and the mouth-watering meal she was tucking in to, she shrugged and said, 'I've been doing some temporary work since leaving a job I'd been in for five years. I thought it would be a good idea to come somewhere quiet and have a think about what I want to do if I have to move on.' *If Lorna's company folds and I have to apply for something more permanent,* she thought, and prayed for Lorna and Josh's sake that it wouldn't come to that. Though they *had* been facing a lot of problems recently.

He nodded, whether in approval or simply in response to what she had said she wasn't sure. Positioning himself on the crate from which he had retrieved his plate, he said, 'You mean you're… what is it you call it…?' He pretended to search for the word. 'Freelance?'

Brows drawn together, Kayla said hesitantly, 'Loosely speaking.' Filling in for Josh and Lorna when she'd been at her worst, after their bookkeeper had suddenly taken off with someone she'd met on the internet, was simply helping two people she cared about a great deal.

Leonidas reached around him for a stoneware vessel that was standing on an old tree stump beside him, hooking his thumb through the handle and bringing it over his shoulder like some ancient warrior at a feast before offering some to Kayla.

A hunter, she ruminated. Like those warring Greeks who had fought to keep their lands from invading Romans. Clever. Living by his wits. Untamed.

'It's homemade and non-alcoholic. Try it,' he invited smoothly, thinking that if 'loosely speaking' meant skirting around the truth then the local wine would have been much better at loosening her tongue to his advantage. However, she was driving, and he had to maintain some responsibility for that. 'What were you doing in your job?' he persevered after she'd nodded her assent, reining in the desire to curb the small talk and cut straight to the chase.

'Accounts. I'm a qualified bookkeeper,' she answered, taking the glass he had filled for her and trying a sip. It tasted zesty and refreshing, with lime and other citrus juices blended with something that made it fizz. 'Why are you smiling like that?' If one could call that curious twist to his mouth a *smile,* Kayla thought.

Because that's about as unlikely as my being a nightclub singer, Leonidas considered, amazed and amused by what he decided must be barefaced lies.

'You don't *look* like a bookkeeper,' he remarked, studying her unashamedly in view of the yarn she

was spinning him. Beautiful long hair and capti-
vating features. Elegant swan-like neck, small but
alluring figure. What he didn't expect was the hard
desire that kicked through his body, mocking his
efforts to remain in command even as he acknowledged her reaction in the colour that stole across
her fine translucent skin.

'What's a bookkeeper supposed to look like?'
she queried with a betraying little wobble in her
voice, feeling his gaze like a hot brand over her
scantily clad body and bare legs.

'Not blonde, beautiful and way too intrusive for
her own good.'

She laughed nervously at his double-edged com-
pliment, feeling a stirring in her blood that had
nothing to do with the zesty punch, the good food,
or the way the warm wind was sighing through the
silver leaves of an olive tree that stood at the edge
of the shady terrace above the overgrown garden.

'What about you?' she asked quickly, to try and
stem the ridiculous heat that was pulsing through
her veins. 'I thought this place was derelict. How
long have you lived here?' She glanced up at the
house, which she had believed was uninhabited.
Most of it was in a serious state of disrepair, but
one wing of the old building looked as if it had

been renovated in recent years. 'I take it you *do* live here?'

'For the time being,' he said uncommunicatively, adding after a moment or two, 'I thought it would be as good a place as any to…what is the expression…? Bed down for a while.'

'You mean…you're just bumming around?'

Leonidas laughed, showing strong white teeth, and through the thick fringes of his lashes he surveyed the young woman sitting opposite him with guarded circumspection, wondering how far she was planning to carry this little charade. Yesterday she had displayed all the characteristics of an opportunity-grabbing undercover reporter, and again this morning, when she had wandered in here with that infernal camera—even if she *had* seemed genuinely distressed when she'd leaped into that hot, angry tirade about her phone, her fridge and her supposedly broken-down car. But if his suspicions about her were right—and he had little reason to doubt that they were—then from the questions she was asking and her response to the answers he was giving he had to admit that she was one hell of a good actress.

'I prefer to call it opting out,' he stated laconically.

'So…do you work?' Kayla enquired.

'When I need to.' Which was twenty-four-seven a lot of the time, he thought grimly. If she was here intent on making a killing out of the Vassalio name, then she would know that already.

And if she wasn't…

If she wasn't, he thought, irritated, refusing to give any credence to that possibility, then she shouldn't have inflicted herself upon him in the way she had.

'And what do you do? For a living, I mean?'

She was still treading cautiously, still playing the innocent. If she'd been trying for an Oscar, Leonidas thought, she would have won it hands-down.

'I'm in construction.' *As you probably well know,* he tagged on silently.

'A builder!' Kayla interpreted, realising her assessment of him was right. He *was* a man who worked with his hands.

'Loosely speaking.' Deliberately Leonidas lobbed her own phrase back at her. Playing along with her whatever her game was, he thought with increasing annoyance. And suddenly he was fed-up with pussyfooting around.

Slinging his plate onto the table, he stood up, thrusting his hands into his pockets, intimidation in his stance and every hard inch of him as he said grimly and with lethal softness, 'OK, Kayla. This has gone far enough.'

'What has?'

He had to hand it to her. She looked and sounded perplexed. He might even have said shocked.

'The charade is over, sweet girl.'

'What charade?' Kayla didn't have a clue what he was talking about. 'I don't understand…'

'Don't you?' He laughed rather harshly. 'Do you think I don't know what your little game is? Don't know why you're here?'

'No.' She had leaped to her feet and stood facing him now with her hands on her hips, her eyes wide and contesting. 'You've obviously got me mixed up with somebody else! I don't know who you think I am, but whoever it is I'm not the person you were expecting.'

'I was hardly *expecting* anyone—least of all another blood-sucking female with her own self-motivated agenda! Unless you're going to tell me you've come all this way by yourself to slap a petition on me as well!'

'No, I haven't!' Kayla riposted, wondering what the hell he was talking about. 'And whatever your problem is—whoever it is you've come here to escape from—I'd appreciate it if you didn't take it out on *me!*'

She was gone before he could utter another word.

CHAPTER THREE

IT WAS THE crash that woke her.

Or had it been the rain and thunder? Kayla wondered, scrambling, terrified, out of bed. She had been tossing and turning in a kind of half-sleep for what seemed like hours, although it might only have been minutes since the storm began.

Now, as she pulled open her bedroom door, the full force of the gale made her cry out when it almost blew her back into the room. In the darkness she could see an ominous shape lying diagonally across the landing and a gash in the sloping roof, which was now open to the wind and the driving rain.

Kayla gasped as lightning ripped across the sky, so close that the almost instantaneous crash of thunder that followed seemed to rock the foundations of the house.

Fumbling to turn on the light switch, she groaned when nothing happened.

'Oh, great!'

Finding the chair where she had folded the jeans and shirt she had travelled in two days ago, with trembling hands she hastily pulled them on over her flimsy pyjamas, and then groped around for her bag and the small torch she always carried on her keyring.

Debris was everywhere as she moved cautiously under the fallen tree-trunk. Twisted branches, leaves, twigs and pieces of broken masonry and plaster scrunched underfoot as she picked her way carefully downstairs.

It was as if the whole outdoors had broken in, she thought with a startled cry as another flash of lightning streaked across the sky. The crash that followed it seemed to rock the villa, causing her to panic at the torrent of rain that was coming in on the raging wind.

And then she heard another sound, like a loud hammering on the external door to the villa, and mercifully a voice, its deep tone muffled, yet still breaking through to her through the tearing gale and the rain.

'Kayla! Kayla? Answer me! Are you in there? Kayla! Are you all right?'

The banging persisted until she thought the door was caving in.

Reaching it and tugging it open, she almost cried with relief when she saw the formidable figure of Leon standing there, his fists clenched as though to knock the door down if it wasn't opened. Rain was running down his face and his strong bronzed throat in rivulets.

It took all her will-power not to sink against him as he caught her arm and shouted something urgently in his own language.

'Get out of here! Quickly!' he ordered, reverting to English. 'There's been a landslide further up the mountain. This house might not be safe to stay in.' And as she hesitated, casting an anxious glance at her belongings, 'We'll come back for your things in the morning!' he shouted above the wind and the lashing rain. 'You're coming with me!'

Petrified, rooted to the spot by the sound of splitting timber somewhere close by on the riven hillside, Kayla felt herself suddenly being whipped off her feet. She was only pacified by the realisation that she was in a pair of strong, powerful arms, being held against Leon's sodden warmth as he ran with her to the waiting truck.

He had left the vehicle's lights on, and after he had set her quickly down on the passenger seat Kayla saw him race around the bonnet with his

head bent against the storm, his purposeful phy-
sique only just discernible through the rain-washed
windscreen.

He opened the driver's door, his long hair dripping, and as he climbed into the cab beside her and
slammed the door against the wind she noticed
that his shirt, which was unbuttoned and hanging loose, like his jeans, was soaked through and
clinging to his powerful torso.

'Thank you! Oh, thank you!' Dropping her head
into her hands as the truck started rumbling away,
Kayla couldn't think of anything else to say. 'I
didn't know what was happening!' she blurted
out when she had recovered herself enough to sit
up straight and turn towards him. 'I woke up and
thought the world was coming to an end!'

'It would have been for you,' Leonidas stated
with grim truthfulness, 'if that tree had fallen on
you.'

But it hadn't, she thought gratefully. Nor was she
now exposed to the damage it had caused. Thanks
to *him,* she realised, and wondered how she would
have coped if he hadn't been passing right at that
moment.

'What happened?' she queried, baffled, as she

began to gather her wits about her. 'Did you just happen to come by?'

'Something like that,' he intoned, without taking his attention from the zig-zagging mountain road. The truck's wiper blades were barely able to cope even at double-speed with the torrential rain.

At half-past one in the morning?

For the first time noticing the clock on the dashboard, Kayla realised exactly what the time was. Had he been out late, seen what had happened as he had driven past? Or had he been in bed? Had he heard the landslide and driven down especially?

Of course not, she thought, dismissing that last possible scenario. No man she knew of would be so gallant as to risk his own safety for a girl he didn't even know let alone like. And it was patently obvious from her two previous meetings with him that he clearly didn't like her. Or *any* of her sex, if it came to that!

'Why are you doing this if you think I'm someone who's out to make trouble for you?' she enquired pointedly, her hair falling, damp and dishevelled, around her shoulders.

'What would you have preferred me to do?' Every ounce of his concentration was still riveted on the windscreen. 'Leave you there to swim? Or worse?'

Kayla shuddered as she interpreted what 'worse' might easily have meant.

'Is it always like this on these islands?' she queried worriedly, staring out at the truck's powerful headlights cutting through the sheets of rain.

'If you come here in the spring it's a chance you take,' he returned succinctly.

Which she had, Kayla thought, deciding that he probably thought her stupid on top of everything else.

'What's likely to happen to the villa?' she asked anxiously, watching the gleaming water cascading off the hills and filling every crack and crevice on the rugged road. 'That tree came right through onto the landing.'

'We'll go down and inspect the damage in the morning.'

'But the furniture and furnishings. And my things,' she remembered as an afterthought. 'Everything's going to get wet.'

'Only to be expected,' he answered prosaically, changing gear to take a particularly sharp bend. 'With a hole in the roof.'

A hysterical little laugh bubbled up inside of her.

Nerves, she decided. And shock. Because there was certainly nothing funny about the havoc this storm had wreaked upon the little Grecian retreat her friends had worked so hard for.

'What am I going to say to Lorna?' She was worrying about how she was going to break the news to her, thinking aloud. 'She and Josh have got enough problems as it is.' And then it dawned on her. 'Oh, heavens!' she breathed, still shaking inside from her ordeal. 'Where on earth am I going to stay? Tonight? Tomorrow? At all?'

'Well, tonight you're going to stay with me,' he told her in a tone that was settled, decisive. 'And tomorrow, when you've telephoned your friend to let her know what has happened, we'll think of something else.'

We, he'd said, as though they were in this thing together. Which they weren't, Kayla thought. Yet strangely she gleaned some comfort from it—along with a contradictory feeling of being indebted to him, too.

'Like what?' She didn't know where to begin, or even if the island had any other suitable or affordable accommodation. Lorna had offered to let her stay in the villa rent-free, and although Kayla had insisted on paying her, it was still only a nominal amount. The alternative was that she could fly home…

'There are three hotels on this side of the island. One of them—the largest—is closed for refurbishment,' Leon was telling her, 'but I'm sure as it's out of season one of the other two will be able to accommodate you.'

'I can't stay with you tonight,' she informed him. 'It's such an imposition, for one thing.' She didn't even *know* him! And from what she had seen of him over the past couple of days neither did she want to. 'You said yourself you wanted to be left alone.'

'Which you've failed to acknowledge since the day you arrived,' he told her dryly. 'So why break with tradition?'

'I'm sorry.' Now she felt even worse. 'You don't have to do this. I'm only making a nuisance of myself…'

'What would you prefer me to do?' he asked. 'Put you out into the storm?' He laughed when he saw the anxiety creasing her forehead. 'Relax,' he advised. 'You're coming back with me. So, no more arguments to the contrary—and definitely no more apologies. Understood?'

Uneasily, Kayla nodded.

'I didn't hear you,' he stated over the rumble of the engine and the jaunty rhythm of the wiper blades trying to keep pace with the interminable rain.

'Understood!' she shouted back, and kept her gaze on the windscreen and her hands in her lap until he brought them safely off the road and onto the paved area of the old farmhouse.

The part of the house he led her into was re-markably clean and tidy. It was surprisingly well-furnished too, even though most of the furniture looked worn and in need of replacing, and the tap-estries on two of the walls, like the once colour-fully striped throws over the easy chairs, were faded from the sunlight and with age. But with its whitewashed walls and cool stone floors it had an overall rustic charm that offered more comfort than she had imagined from the outside.

She was too tired and weary from her experi-ences to take too much interest in how he was liv-ing, and said only after a cursory glance around her, 'I'm really not happy about this.'

She didn't know anything about him, for a start, even if he *had* just rescued her from a house that might possibly be unsafe. He was still a stranger, and up until now a decidedly hostile one.

'I'm afraid you've no choice,' he told her, opening a cupboard and pulling out towels and spare bedlinen, 'because I've no intention of trying to find you a hotel tonight. No hotelier would welcome you turning up at this hour—even if it were safe enough to do so. And if you really don't profess to know me—' He broke off, his speculative gaze raking over her as if, by some miracle, he was at last beginning to believe her. 'I'm not a criminal,' he stated. 'Unless, of course, the police want to charge me with some driving offence I don't yet know about.'

Kayla smiled, relaxing a little, as he had intended her to.

Clever, she thought. Clever and probably very manipulative, she decided, but was too tired to worry about that tonight.

After she had declined his offer of any refreshment, and the room he showed her into was rustic but practical, with the same weary air about its furnishings. Like downstairs, the walls looked as though they hadn't been whitewashed in a long time. A big wooden bed took pride of place, and from the few masculine possessions scattered around the room she gathered that *he* had been using it up until now.

'I'm afraid it isn't five-star, but it's warm and dry and the sheets are clean.' They looked it too. Crisp and white, if a little rumpled, and there was a definite indentation in the plump and inviting-looking pillow. 'Well, I was only in them for half an hour,' he enlightened her, with his mouth tugging down at one side.

So he had been to bed and got up again—which could only have meant that he must have driven down in the storm especially.

'Think nothing of it,' he advised dismissively as their eyes clashed.

Kayla wanted to say something, to thank him at the very least for deserting his bed in the middle of the night to come and see if she was all right. But his manner and all that had gone before kept her mute.

'What will *you* do?' she enquired, glancing down at the bed he'd given up for her. Suddenly worried that she might have given him the wrong idea, quickly she tagged on, 'That wasn't meant to sound like...'

'It didn't,' he said, although the way his gaze moved disconcertingly over her body did nothing to put her at ease. 'Don't worry about me.' He'd started moving away. 'There's a perfectly adequate sofa in the living room.'

Adequate, but not comfortable. Not for his manly size. She had noticed it on the way through and thought now that it wouldn't in any way compensate for losing the roomy-looking bed he'd imagined he would be occupying.

'I really feel awful about this.'

'Don't,' he replied. 'I'm sure you're used to better. As I said, it isn't five-star.' His tone, however, was more cynical than apologetic, and a little dart of rebellion ran through her as their eyes met and locked.

She didn't tell him that she had had a taste of luxurious living and it wasn't something she was keen to get back to. Not when it had meant accompanying Craig to company dinners and luxury conference weekends where she had watched her ex paying homage, she realised now, to people he merely wanted to impress—people he knew could further his corporate ambitions—without really liking them at all.

'I'm more than grateful for—' A sudden vivid flash, accompanied by a deafening crack, had her cutting her sentence short with a startled cry.

'It's all right,' he said. His voice came softly from

somewhere close behind her as the thunder seemed to reverberate off the very walls. 'This house might look as though it's seen better days, but I can assure you, Kayla, the roof is sound. No tree is going to fall in on us, I promise you.'

Her visible fear had brought him over to her. She only realised it as she felt his hands on her shoulders through the thin fabric of her shirt, warm and strong and surprisingly reassuring in view of his previous attitude towards her.

'I'm all right.' She took a step back and his hands fell away from her. She wondered what was most unsettling. The storm—or the touch of this stranger whose bedroom she was unbelievably standing in.

'Of course you are,' he said. 'But get out of those damp clothes. And get a good night's rest,' he advocated, before leaving her to it.

He was right about her clothes being damp, she realised with a little shiver after he had gone. Just the short journey from the villa to the truck and then from the truck to this house had been enough to soak her shirt and jeans. She was grateful to peel them off.

There were a few moments in the king-sized bed when she wondered what she was doing there, unable to keep her thoughts from the man who must have been lying there not more than an hour before. Had he been lying here naked? She felt a sensual little tingle, and her nostrils grasped the trace of a masculine shower gel beneath the scent of fresh linen. But it was only for a few moments, because when she opened her eyes again the tearing winds and driving rain had ceased and a fine blade of sunlight was piercing the dimly shaded room through a slit in the shutters.

Scrambling out of bed, Kayla went over and flung them back, feeling the heat of the sun on her scantily clothed body as it streamed in through windows that were already open to the glittering blue of the sky.

The bedroom overlooked the front yard, the dirt track and the rolling hillside that descended so sharply, with the mountain road, to the blue and silver of the shimmering sea.

She could see the truck parked there on the flagstones, where Leon had left it in the early hours.

A surge of heat coursed through her as she thought about how he had come to her rescue last night, and how helpless she had felt in those hostile yet powerful arms as they had carried her to that truck when she had been too shocked and too bewildered to move.

'So you're awake.' A familiar deep voice overlaid with mockery called out to her as if from nowhere.

Startled, Kayla realised that he had been doing something to his truck. She hadn't noticed until he had pulled himself up from under it.

Uncertainly she lifted a hand, mesmerised for a moment by the shattering impact of his hard, untrammelled masculinity.

With his hair wild as a gypsy's, and in a black vest top and cut off jeans, he looked like a man totally uninhibited by convention. Self-sufficient and self-ruling. A man who would probably shun the constraints that Craig and his company cronies adhered to.

But this man was looking at her with such unveiled interest that her stomach took a steep dive as she realised why.

She was wearing nothing but her coffee and cream lace-edged baby doll pyjamas and, utterly self-conscious, she swiftly withdrew from the window, certain she wasn't imagining the deep laugh that emanated from the yard as she hastily pulled the shutters together again.

The bathroom was, as she'd discovered last night, clean and adequately equipped. Some time this morning a toothbrush, still in its packaging, had been placed upon two folded and surprisingly good-quality burgundy towels on a wooden cabinet beside the washstand. Impressed, silently Kayla thanked him for that.

Fortunately her hairbrush had been in her bag when she had made her hasty exit from the villa last night, along with a spare tube of the soft brown mascara she had remembered to buy before leaving London.

Never one to wear much make-up, she had nonetheless always felt undressed without her mascara. A combination of pale hair and pale eyelashes made her look washed-out, she had always thought, and Craig had agreed.

A sharp, unexpected little stab of something under her ribcage had her catching her breath as she thought about Craig, but surprisingly it didn't hurt as she reminded herself that what Craig Lymington thought wasn't important any more.

Leon was in the large sitting room off the hall, locking something away in a drawer, when Kayla came down feeling fresh and none the worse for her experiences of the previous night.

He was superb, she thought reluctantly from the doorway, noticing how at close quarters the black vest top emphasised his muscular torso, how perfectly smooth and contoured were his arms, their hair-darkened skin like bronze satin sheathing steel. She was pleased she'd put mascara on, and that when she'd brushed her hair forward and then tossed it back, as she always did, it had looked particularly full and shiny this morning.

He looked up and his gaze moved over her. He was clearly remembering what she had looked like at the window earlier.

'I've been trying to ring Lorna but I can't get a signal,' she said quickly, hoping he hadn't noticed the way she'd been ogling him. 'Is it all right if I use your landline?'

'You could—if it was connected,' he returned. He took his own cell phone out of his pocket and handed it to her as she came into the room. It felt smooth and warmed by his body heat, reminding her far too easily of how *she* had felt being held against his hard warmth the previous night.

'As soon as it's a respectable enough time,' she began, while trying to deal with how ridiculously she was allowing him to affect her, 'and after you've dropped me off at the villa, do you think you could point me in the direction of the nearest hotel?'

'One thing at a time,' he advised her. 'The first thing is not to plan anything on an empty stomach.'

'Is that your philosophy on life?' She struggled to speak lightly, which was difficult when there was so much tension in her voice.

'One of them,' he answered, with his mouth tugging down at one corner.

She wondered what the others were, but decided against asking. For all the hospitality this man had shown her, he didn't welcome too much intrusion into his personal life, and Kayla certainly felt as though she had intruded enough.

Surprisingly, she got through to Lorna's office on the first try. Gently, Kayla broke the news to her about the storm and the tree coming down, wanting to spare her friend as much distress as she could. Lorna and Josh had been trying for a baby for quite some time, and Lorna had had two miscarriages in the past two years. Now she was well into the second trimester of another pregnancy, and Kayla regretted having to cause her any more stress as she concluded, 'I haven't had a chance to look at it in daylight, but we're going down after breakfast to assess the damage.'

'We?' Lorna echoed inquisitively, so that Kayla

was forced to gather her wits together in order to avoid any awkward questions.

'Someone from a neighbouring property. They took me in for the night,' she explained, taking care not to even suggest that 'they' was really 'he'. She wasn't ready to be bracketed with another man in her life just yet.

'Then tell them that I can't thank them enough for taking care of my friend.' True to character, Lorna seemed more concerned about Kayla than about the tree crashing down on her precious villa. 'I'm so glad there was someone else there! What would you have done otherwise?'

My thoughts exactly, Kayla mused, unable to keep her eyes from straying to Leon's superbly broad back as he moved lithely out of the room while her friend made plans for what she intended to do.

'Lorna's parents are going to come over and sort out what needs doing,' Kayla reported to him a few minutes later, having found him in the huge and very outdated farmhouse kitchen at the end of the hall. It contained a dresser and a huge wood-burning stove over which Leon was busily wielding a frying pan. A large pine table stood in the centre of the room, already laid for one. Two large-paned windows faced the front of the house, offering stupendous views of the distant sea, while two more on the other side of the room looked out onto the terraced gardens. 'Lorna and Josh have their own business and don't have much free time,' she explained, handing him back his phone, which he casually slipped into the back pocket of his jeans.

Unlike you, Kayla thought, and for a moment found herself envying his flexible lifestyle. His free spirit and total autonomy. The complete lack of binding responsibility.

'Have you always been so self-sufficient?' she asked, watching him cutting melon, which he put on the table beside a plate of fresh pineapple slices. She wondered if he had already eaten or just wasn't bothering.

'I like to think so,' he responded, without looking at her. 'I've always believed—' and found out the hard way, Leonidas thought, his features hardening '—that if you want something done properly there's no surer way but to do it yourself.'

'Another of your philosophies?' Kayla enquired, her hand coming to rest on the back of one the pine chairs and her head tilted as she waited for an answer, which never came.

No man was an island, so the saying went. But

Kayla had the distinct impression that this man was—emotionally, at any rate. He seemed more detached and aloof from the rat race and the big wide world than anyone she had ever met. Uncommunicative. Guarding his privacy like a precious jewel.

'Who did you think I was when you accused me of playing some game with you yesterday?'

'It isn't important,' he intoned, moving back to the stove.

'It seemed to be very important at the time,' Kayla commented, still put out by the names he had called her. 'The things you said to me weren't very nice.'

'Yes, well…we can all make mistakes,' Leonidas admitted, adding freshly chopped herbs to the sizzling frying pan and beginning to accept that he might have made a gross error of judgement in treating her so unjustly. 'I came here to relax. I didn't expect some uninvited young woman with a camera to be taking secretive photographs of me. When you realised I'd seen you on the rocks and you ran from me I decided that you must definitely be up to no good.'

So he had charged at her like an angry bull,

Kayla thought, wondering what he'd thought she was hiding that had incensed him so much.

'Yesterday,' he went on, 'when I invited you to lunch, it was to try to find out why.'

'You accused me of spying on you,' she reminded him, folding her arms in a suddenly defensive pose as she bit back the urge to remind him that she hadn't been trying to photograph him on that beach. 'What did you imagine? That I was some sort of secret agent or something?' she suggested with an ironic little laugh. 'Or a private investigator, hired by a jealous wife—?' She broke off as a more plausible possibility struck her. 'A wife who's taken you to the cleaners and who's still hoping to uncover the hidden millions you haven't told her about that you've got stashed away somewhere? Gosh! Is that it?' she exclaimed, when she saw the way his dark lashes came down over his unfathomable eyes, wondering if she'd hit the nail on the head. 'Not about the millions. I mean…'

'About the wife?'

She nodded. Why else would he have referred to her as a blood-sucking female yesterday? He must be licking his wounds after a very nasty divorce.

'Nice try,' he said dryly, the muscles in his wonderfully masculine back moving as he worked.

'I'm sorry to have to shoot down such a colourful and imaginative story, but I'm not married. And since when did a man simply wanting to protect his privacy mean there's an avaricious and avenging wife in tow?'

'It doesn't,' Kayla answered, wondering why the discovery of his marital status should leave her feeling far more pleased than it should have. 'It just seemed a little bit of an overreaction, that's all,' she murmured, feeling her temperature rising from the way he was looking at her—as though he knew what baffling and unsettling thoughts were going through her head.

'So how did you know about this house?' she asked, since it was apparent now that it wasn't just a deserted building he'd happened to stumble across.

'I was born on this island,' he said, in a cool, clipped voice. 'I have the use of this place when I want it.'

'Who owns it?' she enquired, looking around.

'Someone who is too busy to take much interest in it,' he answered flatly, suddenly sounding bored.

'What a pity,' Kayla expressed, looking around her at the sad peeling walls. 'It could be nice if it was renovated. Someone must have treasured it once.'

Once, Leonidas thought, when its warm, welcoming walls had rung with his mother's beautiful singing. When he hadn't been able to sleep for excitement because his grandfather was taking him fishing the following day...

'Obviously the current owner doesn't share your sentimentality about it,' he remarked, and found it a struggle to keep the bitterness out of his voice.

'You said you were born on this island?' Kayla reminded him, feeling as though she was being intrusive again, yet unable to stop herself. Even less could she envisage him as a helpless, squalling infant. 'It's idyllic. What made you leave?'

His features looked set in stone as he tossed two slices of bubbling halloumi cheese onto slices of fresh bread, topping them with rich red sun-dried tomatoes before he answered, 'I believed there was a better life out there.'

'And was there?'

Again he didn't answer.

But what sort of satisfaction was there in never settling anywhere? Kayla wondered now. In just drifting around from place to place?

'Eat your breakfast,' he ordered, putting the meal on the table in front of her. 'And then we'll go down and inspect the storm damage.'

CHAPTER FOUR

THE STRUCTURE OF the villa had sustained less damage than Kayla had feared. However, after Leon had helped her to clear up the debris and mess caused by the falling tree, it was still a far cry from what it had been when she had arrived.

'I'll have to look for somewhere else,' she accepted defeatedly, trying to sound braver and less anxious than she was feeling as she dropped the last packet of ruined food into a refuse bag.

'My very next step,' Leonidas assured her, taking his phone out of his pocket.

He had changed into a pale blue shirt and jeans before leaving the farmhouse earlier and, looking up from the bag she was tying, Kayla noticed how his rolled-up sleeves emphasised the dark olive of his skin and the virility of his strong arms.

'I think you've done quite enough already,' she reminded him. Not only had he rescued her from a terrifying situation last night, he had given her food and shelter, driven her back here, and then refused to leave when it came to the clean-up operation. 'I'm indebted enough to you as it is!'

'If that's all that's worrying you—forget it,' he drawled. 'I'm not likely to be extracting payment any time soon.'

'That's not funny,' she scolded, still unhappy about being in his debt. Or was it that mocking glint in his eyes that affected her more than his hostility?

Whatever it was, she thought, he unsettled her as no man had ever unsettled her in her life. Not to this degree anyway, she realised. And there was more to it than just the danger of getting too involved with a man whom, until the day before yesterday, she had never even met. It was the potent attraction this man held for her, purely physical in its nature and stronger than any she had felt before. Which was illogical, she decided, when she had been engaged to Craig and fully intending to spend the rest of her life with *him.*

But Leon was already taking the necessary steps to get her fixed up with an alternative place to stay.

Listening to that deep voice speaking in Greek to some hotelier on the other end of the line, Kayla realised how much more difficult it would have been for her if she had been left to find accommodation herself. There would have been the language barrier to overcome for a start.

Now, though, as he came off the phone, Kayla saw him shaking his head. 'I'm afraid they're fully booked for the next three weeks.'

There were three hotels on the island, he had informed her, one closed for refurbishing, and he was now ringing the second one on his list. But again he was shaking his head as he finished speaking to their last possible hope. 'They said they would have had a room if you had telephoned yesterday, but they've had to close this morning because of flooding in part of the hotel last night.'

She could tell that he was almost as dumbfounded as she was.

'Well, that's that, then,' she said, swinging the bin bag up off the tiled floor. 'I'll just have to make the best of it here until Lorna's parents arrive tomorrow.' And after that… She gave a mental shrug as she crossed the tiny kitchen. Who knew?

Watching the determined squaring of her shoulders as he tried to relieve her of the bag, Leonidas felt his heart going out to her.

'Don't be ridiculous,' he said as she opened the door to the garden. 'You can't stay here.' The tree was leaning across the landing at a precarious enough angle to be a safety hazard. Also, because of the galleried landing, the ground floor was open to the elements, as well as to any more debris from the fallen tree.

'No?' Kayla said, coming in from dumping the bag outside. 'And I suppose you can come up with a better idea?'

'Yes, I can,' he stated pragmatically. 'You will stay with me.'

Not can. *Will,* Kayla noted, which marked him as a man who usually got his own way.

'With you?' He was leaning against the sink with his thumbs hooked into his waistband, looking very determined, and a little bubble of humourless laughter escaped her. 'Now look who's being ridiculous,' she accused.

'If you think I'm leaving you here, with that tree likely to come down on you at any moment,' he said, with an upward toss of his chin, 'you can think again.'

'I'm not your responsibility or your problem, Leon,' she stressed trenchantly. 'Anyway, I came here to be alone.'

'Why, exactly?' Leonidas was regarding her with hard speculation. 'What is a girl like you doing on her own in a quiet and remote place like this when you could be enjoying the company of other people your age and living it up somewhere like Crete or Corfu? And don't tell me that you are simply soaking up the sun while considering your next career move, because you could have gone anywhere to do that.'

'Perhaps I don't want to be "living it up",' Kayla replied, feeling pressured by his unwavering determination. 'I came here for peace and quiet. Not to share with anyone else.'

'So did I,' he reminded her, in a way that suggested that the best-laid plans didn't always turn out as one would expect.

'Exactly! And the last thing you want is a… what did you call me? Oh, yes—a "blood-sucking female with her own self-motivated agenda" dumped on you!' she quoted fiercely, with both hands planted on her denim-clad hips. 'Well, believe me, this *isn't* on my agenda!'

'All right. So we didn't get off to a very good start. I shouldn't have said those things to you,' he admitted, coming away from the sink. It seemed to constitute some sort of apology. 'But the fact remains that as things stand this place is a potential hazard, and—my responsibility or not—if you think I am going to stand by and let you risk your safety just because of a few ripe phrases on my part yesterday, then you still have a long way to go in assessing my character. I carried you out of here last night and I'll do it again if I have to.' His features were set with indomitable purpose. 'So, are you going to be sensible and swallow your pride and accept that there isn't an alternative?' he asked grimly.

'There's always an alternative,' Kayla said quickly, refusing to accept otherwise—although the thought of him man-handling her out of there when she wasn't being distracted by falling trees and a possible landslide was far too disturbing even to contemplate.

'Like running away?'

Those jet-black eyes seemed to be penetrating her soul, probing down into her heart and digging over her darkest and most painful secrets.

What right did he have to accuse her of running away? Even if she was, it was none of his business! Yet suddenly everything she had suffered over the past weeks, and everything that had gone wrong since she had been here, finally proved too much.

'Who says I'm running away?' she flung at him grievously. 'And if you think that just because I chose to come on holiday by myself, then I could just as easily wonder the same thing about you! And those weren't just a few ripe phrases you used. You were taking out all your woman problems— whatever they are—on *me!* Do you want to know why I'm here on my own? Then put this in your pipe and smoke it! Saturday was supposed to be my wedding day—only the groom decided he'd rather marry somebody else instead! He just kept the same date and the same time at the same church with the same photographer for *convenience*.' She couldn't keep the bitterness out of her voice.

'Because he wanted to marry her in a hurry, al- though he *did* have the decency to let me know she was pregnant before I broke off our engagement three months ago. And if that wasn't enough we all worked at the same company, which is why I had to leave. I live in a small community, so the whole neighbourhood knew about it as well, and I just couldn't stay there and face the humiliation. So if running away because I'm not thick-skinned enough to stand there and throw confetti over my ex-fiancé and his pregnant secretary is wrong, then I'm sorry!' She uttered a facetious little laugh. 'I'll just have to toughen up in future.'

'Forgive me.'

Leonidas's face was dark with contrition. And shock too, Kayla decided, almost triumphantly.

'The man's a…' He called him something in his own language which she knew wasn't very complimentary. 'I spoke without knowing the facts.'

'Yes, you did.' Now she had got it all off her chest she was beginning to feel a little calmer. 'Anyway, it's all history. Water under the bridge. I'm over him now.'

'Are you?'

'Yes, I am,' she asserted, her mouth firming resolutely. 'He kept to everything we'd planned for us—for our day…' Strangely, that was what had hurt the most in the end. 'Even down to the guest list,' she uttered with another brittle little laugh. 'Well, most of it anyway,' she said. 'It's funny how when you're a couple you seem to have a lot of friends. Then when you break up you realise that they weren't really your friends at all. Most of them were Craig's. Acquaintances, really. He didn't have any real friends. They were all company people. People he'd met through his job. Sales reps. Customers. His management team and their wives. The office hierarchy that he liked us to socialise with.'

'You don't sound very enamoured,' Leonidas remarked.

Kayla glanced up to where he was standing with his hands thrust into his pockets, listening with single-minded concentration to all she was saying. 'I'm just angry with myself for not knowing better.'

'How could you?' Those masculine brows came together in a frown. 'How could anyone prepare for something like that happening?'

'Oh, I had a good tutor, believe me. Dad did the very same thing to Mum—ran off with his secretary. So it wasn't as though I wasn't forewarned. I just wouldn't listen. I thought it could never happen to me. But now I know never to get mixed up with that type of man again.'

'And what type is that?'

'The type with a nicely pressed suit and a spare clean shirt in the office closet. The type who's always late home because his workload's so heavy. The type who thinks every reasonably attractive female colleague is only there to boost his ego.'

Leonidas's dark lashes came down over his eyes, but all he said was, 'I thought that kind of male chauvinism went out with the nineteen-seventies.'

'Oh don't you believe it!' Kayla returned censoriously. She was mopping water from the fridge with all the venom she felt towards Craig Lymington and his kind. 'There's something that happens to a man when he gets behind a desk, gets himself a secretary and has his name on the door. Something he thinks sets him outside the boundaries of accepted moral behaviour. But I'm not going to bore you with that. It's my problem and I should have known better. I didn't want to know and I paid for it. End of story.'

Leonidas doubted somehow that it *was* the end of the story, and reminded himself never to tell her what he really did for a living.

'You've had a tough time,' he accepted, deciding that this damsel in distress who had been so badly treated by her fiancé would probably feel nothing but contempt for him if she knew more about him.

She would instantly bracket him with the type of man she despised. And if for one moment he did let on who he was, he had learned enough about her already to know that she would want nothing to do with him. She would refuse his help—no matter how desperately she needed it—which would do nothing to get her out of the predicament she was in now.

'However,' he continued, 'the most pressing problem you have right now is where you're going to sleep tonight. As I've already said, I wouldn't dream of allowing you to talk yourself into thinking it's all right to stay here…' No matter how far outside the boundaries of morality she might think he was if she knew about his desk and his secretary and the spare shirts he kept in his Athens and London offices. 'Which means you either sleep out in the open or you come back with me. Unless, of course, you're thinking of returning home?'

Almost imperceptibly Kayla flinched. With the villa unusable and nowhere else to stay, it did seem the most feasible thing to do. But if she did, what would she be going back to? Her mother's smugness over having been right about Craig? The neighbourhood's silent sympathies? The whispered comments behind her back? What would everyone say if they realised that not only had her proposed wedding turned out to be non-existent but also that the holiday she had been determined to take on her own had turned into a disaster as well?

'If it's your modesty you are worrying about, and you're thinking I might try and—what is the phrase you English use?—"take advantage" of you,' Leon said, remembering, 'then I must assure you that I wouldn't contemplate trying to seduce a girl who is on the rebound.'

'I'm *not* on the rebound,' Kayla denied hotly. But then, realising that he might take that to mean she wanted him to take advantage of her, she added quickly, 'I mean…' And then ran out of words because she didn't know how to phrase what she was trying to convey.

'I know what you mean,' he said, making it easy for her, although there was a sensual mockery on that devastating mouth of his that had her wondering just how pleasurable his taking advantage of her might be, if she were so inclined to let him.

'So what's it to be, Kayla?'

Her name dripped from his lips like ambrosia from the lips of Eros, although she doubted that even the Greek god of love could have harboured the degree of sensuality this man possessed.

She didn't want to go home, that was for sure. Yet neither did she want to be indebted to a total stranger—even if he did look like the answer to every woman's darkest fantasy! That didn't alter the fact that he was a stranger, and no woman in her right mind would agree to stay with a man she didn't even know. So where did that leave her? she asked herself. On the ground outside?

Very quietly, Leonidas said, 'Pack a bag and come with me.'

'You know I can't stay with you.'

'I'm not going to try and talk you into it. Pack a bag,' he instructed again, without offering her any idea of what his plans were. 'I'll finish mopping up here.'

Leon had asked her to follow him in the car. The little hatchback coughed a few times when Kayla tried to start it, which brought him over from the cab of his truck to investigate.

The engine fired into life just as he was approaching the bonnet.

Looking up at him through the car's open window with a self-satisfied glint in her eyes, Kayla asked, 'Do you believe me now?'

That masculine mouth pulled to one side, although he made no verbal response. Perhaps he was a man who didn't like being reminded of his mistakes too often, Kayla thought, unable to help feeling smug.

'It needs a good run,' he said, speaking with some authority. 'It's probably been standing idle for too long, which isn't good for any car.'

Following his truck down the zig-zag of a mountain road, Kayla was tempted to stop and take in the breathtaking views of the sea and the sun-drenched hillsides. But she kept close behind Leon's truck, envying his knowledge of every sharp bend, admiring the confidence and safety with which he negotiated them.

After guiding her down past a cluster of white-washed cottages, he pulled up outside another, with blue shutters and, like the rest, pots of gaily coloured flowers on its veranda.

'Since you refuse to stay with me, I will have to leave you in the capable hands of Philomena,' Leon told her, having come around the truck to where Kayla was just getting out of the car.

'Philomena?'

'A friend of mine,' he stated, moving past her. 'There is one small snag, however,' he went on to inform her as he swung her small single suitcase out of the boot.

'Oh?' Kayla looked up at him enquiringly as he slammed the lid closed.

'She doesn't speak any English,' he said.

'So why would she want me staying with her?' Kayla practically had to run after him. It was obvious that he wasn't going to allow that rather large drawback—to Kayla's mind, at any rate—to interfere with his plans.

'Her family have all grown up and moved away,'

he tossed back over his shoulder. 'Trust me. She will be very glad of the company of someone else—especially another woman.'

'But have you asked her?' Kayla wasn't sure that anyone—no matter how lonely they might be—would welcome a guest turning up unexpectedly on their doorstep.

'Leave the worrying to me,' he advised, and uneasily Kayla did.

He had said Philomena was a friend, but as he brought Kayla through to the homely sitting room of the little fisherman's cottage without even needing to knock, she calculated that the woman in dark clothes who greeted them with twinkling brown eyes and a strong, character-lined face was old enough to be his grandmother.

Her affection for Leon was clear from the start, but suddenly as they were speaking the woman burst into what to Kayla's ears sounded like a fierce outpouring of objection. The woman was waving her hands in typically European fashion and sending more than a few less than approving glances Kayla's way.

'She isn't happy about my staying here and why should she be?' Kayla challenged, taking in the abundance of framed family photographs and brightly painted pottery and feeling as much mortified as she felt sympathetic towards the elderly woman.

'She's happy, Kayla,' Leonidas told her, breaking off from a run of incomprehensible Greek. He started speaking very quickly in his own language again, which brought forth another bout of scolding and arm-waving from a clearly none-too-pleased Philomena.

'I'm sorry,' Kayla apologised through the commotion, hoping the woman would understand as she picked up her suitcase and starting weaving through the rustic furniture towards the door.

'No, no! No, no!' A lightly restraining hand came over Kayla's arm. 'You stay. Stay Philomena, eh?' The look she sent Leonidas shot daggers in his direction. Her voice, though, as she turned back to Kayla, was softer and more encouraging, her returning smile no less than sympathetic as a workworn, sun-dappled hand gently palmed Kayla's cheek. 'You come. Stay.'

A good deal of gesticulation with a far warmer flow of baffling Greek seemed to express the woman's pleasure in having Kayla as her guest.

'You see,' Leonidas remarked, looking pleased

with himself as Philomena drew her gently away from the door. 'I said she would want you to stay.'

The appreciative look Kayla gave her hostess turned challenging as she faced the man who had brought her there. 'Then what were you arguing about?' she quizzed.

'Philomena has no one to scold nowadays, so she likes to scold me.' His mouth as he directed a look towards their hostess was pulling wryly. 'Philomena bore seven children, but her one claim to fame, as she likes to call it, is that she delivered me. I'm eternally grateful to her for introducing me to this universe,' he expressed with smiling affection at Philomena, 'but she does tend to imagine that that gives her licence to upbraid me at every given opportunity.'

'For what?' Kayla was puzzled, still not convinced.

One of those impressive shoulders lifted as he contemplated this. 'For leaving the island. For coming back. For not coming back.'

Kayla noted the curious inflexion in his voice as he made that last statement. Her smile wavered. 'And what about just now?'

'Just now?'

Leonidas looked at the woman who had pulled

him screaming into the world. She had been there—never far away—throughout his childhood. A comfort from his father's strict and sometimes brutal regime of discipline, his rock when his mother had died.

'I don't think she's happy with the way I've turned out,' he commented dryly to Kayla, and thought that if it were true he wouldn't blame Philomena. There were times lately, he was surprised to find himself thinking, when he had been far, far from happy with himself.

'Oh?' Kayla clearly wanted to know more, but he had nothing more to offer her.

Gratefully he expressed his thanks to Philomena, adding something else, which brought Kayla's cornflower-blue eyes curiously to his as he started moving away.

'I've told her to take care of you,' he translated, with a blazing smile that made Kayla's stomach muscles curl in on themselves. And that was that. He had gone before she could utter another word.

Kayla settled in to her new accommodation with remarkable ease, and as she had suspected, despite the language barrier, she found Philomena Sarantos to be a warm and generous hostess.

She wondered what Leon had meant about Philomena being unhappy with the way he had turned out. Had he meant because of his lifestyle? Not having a steady job? Because he seemed content to drift from place to place?

Two days passed and she saw nothing of him. But then, what had she expected? Kayla meditated. Hadn't he made it clear from the beginning that he didn't welcome intrusion into his life? And, although he had invited her to stay with him at the farmhouse the morning after that tree had come down, she wondered if it hadn't been merely a hollow gesture on his part. He'd known she would refuse, so he'd been perfectly safe in offering her his roof over her head.

What did it matter? she decided now. She'd had enough to occupy her time without bothering herself about Leon over the past couple of days.

The previous day she had driven up to the villa after Lorna's parents had texted her with the estimated time they would be arriving. They had brought some local men with them who were arranging for the removal of the tree, and someone else who, having inspected the building, pronounced the place off-limits for the time being.

After arranging with the men for the necessary works to be carried out, her friend's parents had been extremely concerned as to where Kayla would stay. But having satisfied them—just as she had done with Lorna, over the phone the previous day—that she had found suitable alternative accommodation, she had seen the couple off to spend a few days on Corfu and—in their own words—'make the whole trip worthwhile'.

Now, with the sun having just risen and another glorious day yawning before her, Kayla traversed the dusty path that led from Philomena's cottage and gasped with delight when it brought her down onto the sun-washed shingle of a secluded cove.

Striding down through the scrub, Leonidas came to where the beach opened out before him and stopped dead in his tracks.

Kayla was wading, shin-deep, in the translucent blue water, moving shorewards. She was looking down into the water and hadn't spotted him yet.

He would have considered the fine white cotton dress she was wearing with its sheer long sleeves and modest yoke demure in any other circumstances, because it made her look almost angelic with her loose blonde hair moving in the breeze. But she had evidently—perhaps unintentionally—

allowed the sea to lap too high to preserve her modesty, for now the garment clung wetly to her body, so that the gold of her skin and her small naked breasts were clearly visible beneath.

As she waded forward the sun struck gold from her hair, illuminating the lustrous gold of lashes that lay against her cheeks as her interest never wavered from the water.

Transfixed by her beauty, he noticed the grace of her movements, the way her progress changed the light, making her breasts appear indistinct one moment and then tantalisingly defined the next. A virginal siren, tantalising enough to set his masculine hormones ablaze as his gaze swept the length of her tunic, which only reached the tops of her slender thighs.

She looked up—and when she saw him she put her hand to her mouth in shock. Then her bare feet were running lightly over the shingle towards the white floppy hat he had only just noticed lying discarded nearby.

'I didn't see you,' she called out, snatching up the hat that had been covering her ever-present camera and the rest of her things lying there on the shingle.

'Evidently not.' He couldn't contain the slow

smile that played across his mouth as he noted the purposeful way she covered her wet top with the hat, her own smile feigning nonchalance, as though she didn't care.

'Have you been standing there long?'

Not nearly long enough, Leonidas thought, struggling to keep control of his unleashed hormones and the effect she was having on him. He was glad he hadn't simply worn bathing shorts, as he'd been tempted to do, and instead had donned linen trousers with a loose, casual shirt.

She had probably had enough of men lusting after her for their own primeval satisfaction—including that fiancé of hers—without having to endure the same kind of treatment from him.

'You shouldn't go bathing like that without a chaperone,' he chided softly, the dark lenses of his sunglasses revealing nothing of his thoughts.

'I didn't mean to.' Beneath the pale swathe of her hair a modestly clad shoulder lifted almost imperceptibly. 'The sea was beckoning me while I was paddling and I just got carried away.'

'It has a way of doing that, and before you know it—' He made a gesture with his hand like a fish taking a dive. 'It's nature drawing us back to itself.'

He saw her golden head tilt and was struck by

the vivid clarity of those cornflower-blue eyes as she surveyed him. 'What a beautiful thing to say.'

Leonidas laughed. 'Was it?' He found himself swallowing and his throat felt dry. He had been accused of expressing himself in many ways in his time, he recalled, but beautifully had never been one of them.

She had turned round to gather her things and was starting to pull on white cropped leggings.

'How are you getting on with Philomena?' he asked.

Thrusting her feet into flip-flops, Kayla retrieved the hat she had momentarily discarded and turned back to face him, keeping its wide brim strategically in place across her breasts.

'She's great.' Her face lit up with genuine warmth. 'She reminds me of my gran.'

'That's good.' He knew he was looking self-satisfied as he flipped open the notebook he'd taken out of the back pocket of his trousers. 'And what does your grandmother think of your being here alone?' He was in danger of sounding distracted, but it was vital he got something down. Something he'd forget if he didn't consign it to paper this very instant. 'Isn't she afraid you'll fall prey to some licentious stranger?'

'No.' Picking up her camera and sunglasses, which she slid onto her head, Kayla pushed a swathe of golden silk back off her shoulder with the aid of the sunscreen bottle she was holding. 'She died. A few months ago.'

The sadness in her voice required nothing less than Leonidas's full attention. 'I'm sorry.'

'Yes. So am I,' Kayla responded, reaffirming his suspicion that she had cared a great deal for her elderly relative.

'You were close?' He didn't even need to ask.

She nodded. 'Mum and I never really were. And after Dad left he was never the loving father type whenever I got to see him, so we just drifted apart over the years. But Gran—Mum's mum— she filled the void in every way she could.'

She was looking over her shoulder out to sea but Leonidas knew that she wasn't seeing the white-crested waves and the indigo blue water. She was hiding emotion—nothing more—because she was embarrassed by it.

'So you lost your fiancé on top of losing a grand-mother?' he commented, with a depth of feeling he wasn't used to. 'That's rough.'

She shrugged. 'At least I had Lorna,' she told

him with a ruminative smile. 'On both counts she was there for me. She helped me through.'

'Tell me about her,' he said somewhat distractedly Kayla thought as she started walking casually a step or two ahead of him, because he was busy scribbling in a notebook.

But she told him anyway, about the friend she had known from her first day at school who had come to mean as much as a sister to her. About the interior design work that Lorna and her husband were involved in, and how brilliant they were at what they did, but how, with the state of the market and then losing their biggest customer, things had become extremely difficult for them recently. She even went on to tell him how she might find herself looking for another job if things didn't improve.

He wasn't really listening, she decided, relieved, feeling that she had gabbled on too much.

'What are you writing?' She stopped on the shingle, turning to him with her chin almost resting on the hat she was still clutching to her beneath her folded arms.

'Just jotting down a few things I don't want to forget.' He had snapped the notebook closed and was stuffing it into his back pocket.

'You were sketching.' Suddenly it dawned. 'You were sketching *me*.'

'Leave it, Kayla.' His words were laced with a warning not to pursue it.

'You were sketching me. Oh, no!' Kayla hid her face in the wide brim of her hat. How could he? With the ends of her hair all lank and dripping, and she wasn't even wearing any mascara, let alone a bra! 'I look like a drowned and lashless rat!'

'You look like an angel,' Leonidas told her, voicing his earlier thoughts.

'You can't be serious!' Kayla protested, bringing her head up, clinging to her crushed hat as her only defence against those shaded yet all-seeing eyes.

'I never joke about beauty. Particularly the beauty of a woman,' he said, in a voice that seemed to trickle with pure honey.

And you would have known scores of those! Known just what to say to make them feel like you're making me feel now, Kayla thought hectically. Weak-kneed and breathless and wanting so much to believe that all he was saying was true!

She pulled a face, and in spite of everything managed to say with a tremulous little laugh, 'Does that line usually work?'

The firm masculine mouth compressed, and

she couldn't seem to drag her gaze from it as he prompted, 'Does it work in what way?' Now that mouth took on a mocking curve. 'In getting you into my bed?'

Kayla felt heated colour steal into her cheeks. Which was ridiculous, she thought. She was hardly a novice to male attention. She'd been planning a wedding, for heaven's sake! Yet there was something about this man that was more exciting and more dangerous to her than any other man she had ever met.

'Isn't it customary?' she returned somewhat breathlessly in answer to his reference to getting her into bed.

'Possibly,' he acceded, 'but not in this case. And not with someone who has been made to feel so unsure of herself that she blushes at the mere mention of a man and woman finding pleasure in each other. Or a man taking any interest in her. There's really no need to hide from me, Kayla.'

Perhaps there wasn't. But when he took the hat she was clutching to her like a shield and his hand accidentally brushed the sensitised flesh above her modest neckline she realised that it was herself that she was afraid of. Of feelings that were too reckless and wild to think about. Purely physical feelings that had surfaced the moment she had first seen him standing on that other beach a few days ago.

Now, with her wet top doing nothing to protect her from his gaze, she could feel her blood starting to surge and the peaks of her breasts tightening in response to his hot regard, so that all she could think about was that hard masculine body locked in torrid sensual pleasure on some bed. And not just any bed. On hers!

'Are you saying that your interest is purely aesthetic?' she queried, her voice croaking from her shaming thoughts and the knowledge of how her rapidly rising breasts were betraying her to him.

'No.' He had removed his sunglasses and was hooking them onto the waistband of his trousers. Now she could see his eyes clearly.

They were dark and heavy-lidded beneath the thick swathe of his lashes, and glittering with such intensity of purpose that her every nerve went into red alert as he closed the screaming distance between them.

CHAPTER FIVE

HIS MOUTH OVER hers was like an Olympic torch blazing into life, setting her insides on fire and sending molten sensations of light searing through her blood.

His kiss was passionate, yet tender. Dominant, yet testing. And the mind-blowing expertise with which he lured her mouth to widen for him was the technique of a man who had studied and understood women—a far cry from a man who had such a laid-back attitude to life. A wanderer. A drifter. Without purpose or design.

He smelled of the earth and of the pines that clad the higher slopes of the hillsides. He was burning with everything wild and unfettered, unrestrained. And yet she felt his restraint—a purposeful holding back—as he held her loosely within the exciting circle of his arms.

That was until the hands that were still clutching her camera and the sunscreen bottle against his wide, cushioning shoulders suddenly slid around his neck. Then, with a groan of defeat, his restraint fell away, leaving only raw passion in its wake as he tossed her hat aside and pulled her hard against him.

Kayla heard a gushing in her ears and wasn't sure whether it was the heavy pounding of her blood or whether she was being captured and submerged beneath the relentless power of the sea.

She could feel the whole hard length of his body—every last inch of it—and she could feel her own responding to the drugging hunger of his mouth.

His back was firm and muscled, and she wished she wasn't encumbered by her possessions so that she could slide her eager hands across it. There was no such encumbrance though in the way her body locked with his. His chest was a wall of thunder, crushing her aching breasts, while the potent evidence of his hard virility was making her pulse with need.

When he put her from him, holding her at arm's length, she uttered a strangled murmur of breathless shock and disappointment.

'Why did you do that?' she quavered. Why had he kissed her when he had just claimed he had no intention of trying to get her into bed?

He was breathing as heavily as she was, and a deep flush was staining the olive skin across the strong, hard structure of his cheeks.

'Because you were wondering what it would be like if I did.'

Still trembling, and perturbed by how easily he could not only read her mind but also by how easily he could bend her to his will, she challenged brittly, 'So why did you stop?'

'Because, as I told you before, I have no intention of taking advantage of a woman on the rebound,' he reminded her, even though his breathing was still laboured and his strong face racked from the passion he was struggling to keep in check.

'And—as I told *you* before—I'm not on the rebound,' Kayla protested adamantly, shamed by her response when he was showing such self-control, and when she seemed to have relinquished all of hers in one experimental kiss!

'Aren't you?' he disputed, although there was a wry smile tugging at one corner of his mouth that softened his challenging remark, before he went on to add, 'You had a relationship with him, didn't you?'

'Well, of course I did,' Kayla returned. 'Of sorts.'

'Of sorts?' He tilted his head, his brows drawing quizzically together. 'How am I supposed to interpret *that?*'

'Any way you like!' Kayla tossed back at him, too embarrassed to tell him that Craig's enthusiasm for her had seemed to go off the boil for several weeks before their break-up, and that she was ashamed of herself now for not suspecting the truth. She had believed him when he had blamed work overload for his not showing enough interest in her. When he'd assured her that things would be different when they were married. When he had got the precious promotion he'd spent all his time working for.

'Were you living with him?'

'No.'

'Why not? If I ever set my mind on a woman I want to become my wife, then she will be firmly in my life—and my bed—before I even ask her.'

'I didn't want us to move in together. Not until we were married,' Kayla emphasised. 'And Craig was in full agreement with that.'

'Really?' Mocking scepticism marked that hard masculine face. 'You could do without each other *that* much?'

'Not that it's any concern of yours,' Kayla pointed out, hating having her relationship with her ex scrutinised so closely by this man she scarcely knew, 'but we wanted to start married life properly. In a place that was our own. I didn't want to just move into his flat. Anyway, there's more to a relationship than jumping into bed with each other at every given opportunity,' she stressed, unconsciously wiping her mouth with the back of her hand. Her lips still felt bruised and swollen and, like her susceptible body, burning from Leon's wholly primal, earth-shattering kiss.

'Is there?' he asked, and she could feel those perspicacious eyes following her involuntary action, mocking her, disconcertingly aware.

'Yes!' She was trembling, knowing that the way she had just behaved with him made nonsense of everything she was saying. And the worst thing was he knew it too. 'The type of man I let myself get involved with doesn't just give in to basic animal lust.'

He chuckled under his breath. 'Is that what I was doing? Then you must forgive me if I fail to live up to the constraints of the type of man you are obviously used to. Although I *could* hazard a guess that your relationship was sadly lacking in what was required to make a lifetime commitment, and that the lack of passion between you could have been why he was getting his satisfaction elsewhere.'

The reminder hurt, stinging her pride and giving rise to that same feeling of inadequacy she had felt after she'd got over the initial blow of Craig's betrayal—especially coming from someone who oozed the sort of sexual potency that this man did.

'I'm sorry,' he murmured, surprising her suddenly. 'I didn't mean to rub it in.'

'Didn't you?' she accused, hiding her hurt pride and dignity beneath the burnished gold of her lowered lashes.

'Well, all right.' A self-effacing smile touched that mouth that had the power to drug her. 'I did. But until it stops hurting, Kayla, you aren't ready for an involvement with any other man. And even if you were, the last thing a sensitive girl like you would want is an involvement with a man like me.'

Why not? Crazily, she heard the mortifying question spring to her lips and was half-afraid that she had actually spoken it. Wasn't he just the type of man she needed right now to drive the bitter aftertaste of Craig and all his shallow-minded smart set out of her mind?

'Believe it or not, I'm not looking for one,' she responded, to assure herself as much as Leon. Well, she wasn't, was she? Wasn't she better off—as her mother had always claimed to be—on her own?

'Sensible girl,' Leonidas drawled and, stooping to pick up her hat, deposited it gently and unceremoniously on her head.

'Thanks.' Kayla pulled a wry face. 'Perhaps you'd like to sketch me like this?' she challenged broodingly, relieved, nevertheless, that the disconcerting subject of her love-life had finally been swept aside.

What wasn't so easy to sweep aside, however, was the memory of what had transpired between them a few moments ago.

Why had she responded to him so shamelessly if, as he'd suggested, she was still affected by what Craig had done? Was she so wanton? So desperate for a man? Any man? she wondered. Might she have let this virtual stranger take her here on the shingle without a thought for how it might leave her feeling afterwards?

'I won't be sketching you at all,' he said dismissively. 'For the simple reason that you are wrong. I'm no artist. But if I were, and if I had to keep looking at you looking like this...' His gaze slid over her tantalisingly wet top, making her quiver inside from the powerful impulses generated by the naked need in his eyes, 'then—old boyfriend or no old boyfriend—I definitely would wind up taking you to bed.'

The climb up through the scrub to Philomena's cottage was hot and hilly, and Leonidas walked ahead of Kayla, protecting her from the dense and thorny vegetation that was encroaching on the narrow path, thriving in the rough terrain.

He had had an exacting morning, sorting out a problem that had arisen back in his London office—a case of divided opinion between a couple of members of his board, which his second-in-command had apologised for bringing to his attention.

They said it was tough at the top, he reminded himself with a grimace. And they could say it again, because no matter how much he needed to escape the rigours of the office for a while, he still needed to keep his finger on the pulsing heart of his business.

Shopping malls, leisure complexes and housing developments didn't build themselves, and after the flak he had taken from the press over the neglect of local residents with last year's bitter fiasco he needed to ensure that no loopholes were left for mercenary lawyers and unprincipled members of his team to make unscrupulous deals over.

Being labelled 'ruthless', 'unscrupulous' and 'a profiteer' by the media wasn't something he wanted repeated any more than he wanted further episodes like the one with his publicity-hungry bed-partner Esmeralda Leigh. He had a reputation to uphold—one that he valued—both in his corporate and his private life, and he would protect and defend it with every shred of his power and his unwavering principles. But he hadn't got where he was today without treading a path that had made him tough, hard-nosed and uncompromising, and he had no intention of wavering from that path. Of allowing himself or anyone else to imagine for one moment that he was going soft. Not even this infernally beautiful girl...

Hearing her breath coming shallowly some way behind him, he stopped and waited for her to catch up. She was clutching her bottle of sunscreen lotion, the bulky camera dangled around her neck, and with her white leggings, her tunic top and that huge floppy hat she looked like an overgrown child who had just raided her great-grandmother's attic. He was happy to notice—for his own sake—that her top had nearly dried.

'Here. Let me carry that.' He could see her cheeks were flushed and that she was finding it a struggle keeping up with him, and he held out his hand for the camera, which she happily relinquished. Silently he extended his other hand.

Realising his intention, Kayla hesitated briefly, and saw a mocking smile touch his sensational mouth.

'It's all right. It doesn't constitute a tacit agreement to let me into your bed,' he advised her dryly.

Of course it didn't, she thought. But an impulse of something so powerfully electric seemed to pass between them when she took his hand that it certainly felt like it.

'Thanks,' she uttered tremulously, hoping that he would think it was the uphill climb in the heat over the rough ground that was making her sound so breathless. Not that every cell was leaping in response to her physical awareness of him just as it had when he had kissed her down there on the beach.

'Where did you learn to speak English so proficiently?' she asked, needing to say something—although she *was* genuinely interested to know.

'When I work, I work mainly in the UK,' he informed her. 'And my grandmother was English, so I had a head start while I was still knee-high to a cricket.'

'Grasshopper.'

'What?' The way he was looking down at her, with such charismatically dark eyes, sent a sensually charged little tingle along Kayla's spine.

'It's knee-high to a grasshopper,' she corrected him, contemplating how well the backdrop of the rugged coast and the meandering hillsides served to strengthen the ruggedness of this man who had been born part of them. But she'd picked up on what he'd just said about *when* he worked. So his employment definitely wasn't regular, she thought, reminded of the recent slump in the building trade and how difficult it had made things for a lot of its workers. Perhaps that was why he'd chosen to 'opt out', as he'd put it, for a while.

'How old were you when you left the island?' She found herself wanting to know much more about him.

'Fifteen.'

She remembered him saying that he'd left to find a better life. 'On your own?' she queried. 'Did you leave to go to college?' she asked, when he didn't answer her question. What else could possibly have taken him away at such a young age?

He laughed at that—a sound without humour. 'No college. No university. I did have hopes of furthering my education, but my father wouldn't hear of it.'

'Why not?' Kayla asked, amazed.

'He wanted me to get out into the world, like he had, and "do an honest job" as he called it.'

'Really?' Kayla sympathised. 'And what did *he* do?'

'He eked a living out of this land,' he told her, with an edge to his voice that had her looking at her curiously.

'And where are they now? Your parents?' She couldn't believe they could still be living on the island, otherwise why would he be staying here alone in some absentee owner's sadly neglected house?

'My parents are dead,' he told her as he walked half a stride ahead of her. There was no emotion now beside that surprisingly hard cast to his mouth.

'I'm sorry,' Kayla murmured. She had discovered during a conversation in the villa with him the other day that he, like Kayla, was an only child.

'One learns to get over these things,' he replied. From the harshness of his tone, however, she wondered if he had. Or was there some other reason, she pondered, for that inexorable grimness to his features?

'Still…you have Philomena,' she said brightly, hoping to lighten the mood. She couldn't understand why down there on the beach he had behaved like an exciting lover and yet now seemed as uncommunicative as ever.

Was it by chance that he had just happened to come across her down there? Or had he come looking for her especially?

A sharp little thrill ran through her at the possibility that he had.

'Did she tell you where I was?'

His disconcerting glance at her took in what she knew was her thoroughly dishevelled appearance, and a lazy smile curved his mouth, instantly transforming his features.

'Are you suggesting I asked her?'

Mortified that he would even think she might have wanted him to, Kayla tried to tug her hand out of his, and sucked in a breath when he refused to let it go.

'Yes, I did,' he admitted easily, without any of the embarrassment that was burning Kayla's cheeks. 'I came down to Philomena's to check on you. You've had a bad experience. I didn't like to think of it ruining your holiday.'

He actually cared?

Well, of course he was concerned for her, she thought, mindful of the lengths he had gone to in rescuing her the other night, and then not only helping her to clean up the villa afterwards but also bringing her to Philomena's as well.

'It hasn't. Thanks,' she offered, grateful to him, and was warmed by a flash of something closely resembling admiration in his eyes.

She wondered if he had a girlfriend or a partner. It certainly seemed he'd had a stormy affair, judging by the way he had referred to her when he had been generalising about her sex the other day.

'Why were you so unfriendly to me when we met those first couple of times?' she queried, suddenly needing to know. 'You still haven't told me.'

She started as he suddenly stopped dead, pulling her round to face him on the path.

'Do you *never* stop asking questions?' he demanded, his face a curious blend of impatience and amusement.

'No.' She gave him a sheepish little look and shrugged her shoulders. 'I'm afraid it's a fault of mine. Apparently, according to my star sign, I was born on "the Day of Curiosity",' she quoted with a little giggle.

'And do you really believe all that stuff?'

Seeing the scepticism marking the strong and perfectly sculpted features, she laughed and said, 'No. But they've got that part of me right!'

'You can say that again,' he remarked dryly. 'And as a matter of interest exactly when *is* this illustrious day?' He made a half-amused sound down his nostrils when she told him. 'So you've just had a birthday?' he observed. 'And how old are you, Kayla?'

'Twenty-three.'

'Old enough to know when a man doesn't welcome any more probing into his private life.'

And that told her, Kayla thought, feeling suitably chastised. This time when she tried to pull her hand away she was even more disconcerted when he allowed her to do so.

They had reached the top of the path that ran up alongside Philomena's cottage. There was an area at the back, with a lime tree and a couple of orange trees, where Philomena also grew aubergines and sweet peppers, and where chickens foraged freely in the open scrub.

'How's the car going?' Leon asked, noticing it parked against the side wall of the cottage.

Still feeling put down, but relieved to be speaking on a much less personal level with him, Kayla murmured, 'Fine.' And suddenly, with tension causing a little bubble of laughter to burst from her, she proclaimed, 'Which is more than can be said for yours!'

His truck was parked on the edge of the dirt road just behind the little hatchback, and she could see that one of its tyres was completely flat.

'Oh, dear!' She tried not to giggle again as he thrust the camera at her and, swearing quietly under his breath in his own language, went to deal with changing the wheel.

Leaving him to it, Kayla wandered into the garden, where Philomena was pegging out some washing, sending a couple of chickens scrambling, clucking noisily.

'A flat tyre.' Kayla made a gesture to indicate what she meant and Philomena nodded, rolling her eyes.

Which meant what? Kayla wondered, curious. Had Philomena hoped that the boy she had brought into the world thirty-odd years ago might be doing better for himself by now? Was that what Leon had meant when he'd said she wasn't happy with the way he had turned out?

Dismissing it from her mind, she moved to help Philomena, but her hostess waved her aside with a warm but incomprehensible protest, pointing to the reclining seats in the welcoming shade of a sun umbrella. Not wishing to offend, Kayla went inside and donned a bikini with matching red and white wrap, which she tied, sarong-style, just above her breasts, before coming back outside into the now deserted garden.

A short time later Philomena emerged from the house with two glasses of something cool and re-freshing—juice for her, Kayla realised gratefully, and something a little stronger for Leon.

'I'll take it out to him,' she volunteered, putting her glass down on a nearby table and leaving a thankful Philomena hurrying back inside, because the telephone had started ringing inside the house.

Her discarded wrap had fallen down behind the chair, and wasn't very easy to reach, so with a little sliver of excitement Kayla left it where it was and proceeded to take the glass to Leon as she was.

For the last twenty-minutes or so her ears had been tuned to every sound coming from the dirt road—from the slamming down of a boot to the chink of metal being laid down on sun-baked stones. Now, as she rounded the corner of the house, Kayla's heart kicked into overdrive.

With his shirt removed, and faded blue jeans having replaced his linen trousers, Leon was crouched down, securing a nut on the spare wheel, and for a few moments Kayla could only stand there, watching him unobserved.

His body was beautiful. The bronzed skin sheathed muscles that were flexing as he worked, revealing the tension in his straining biceps and across his wide shoulders, in the tapering structure of his strong and sinewy back.

'Philomena thought you'd like something to drink,' Kayla told him, dry-mouthed, noticing before he turned around how his hair waved below the nape of his neck like jet against burnished bronze.

He dropped the spanner he was using and stood up, his movements cool and easy. That knowing curve to his mouth suggested that he was well aware of her reluctance to let him think that it was entirely her idea.

'That's very good of her.' His answer and his lopsided smile assured her that two could play at that game. His eyes, however, were tugging over her scantily clothed body in a way that was making her feel naked.

'You've been a long time. You should have let me help you,' Kayla remarked, handing him the glass. The accidental touch of his fingers against hers sent a sharp little frisson through her.

'And do you think I would have achieved much with you looking like that?'

Kayla swallowed, watching him drink, trying not to make it too obvious that she was having difficulty staying unaffected by *his* state of undress.

In fact she was finding it impossible not to allow her gaze free rein over his superb body—from the contoured strength of his smooth chest, with its taut muscles and flat dark nipples, to the black line of hair that started just above his navel and ran down inside the waistband of the denim that encased his flat stomach and narrow hips.

He was like a beautiful sleek stallion. All leanness and rippling muscle, with the power to dominate and excite, to control and to conquer using the pulsing energies and surging potency of his body.

'Do you see what I mean?' he taunted softly.

Yes, she did, and she could feel those energies transmitting their sensual messages along her nerve-endings, tugging shameless responses from every erogenous zone in her body.

Beneath the satiny white cups of her bikini her burgeoning breasts throbbed, sending a piercing arrow of need to the heart of her loins.

He was so raw, so masculine, and so shamelessly virile. She wanted to know what it was like to have a man like him filling her, taking her to the wildest edges of the universe with him while she lay beneath him, sobbing her pleasure, in glorious abandon to his thrilling and governing hands.

Shocked by her thoughts, she tried to shake them away, feigning an interest in his truck to try and restore some sense of propriety in herself, grappling for equilibrium.

'Did this thing come with the house?' she queried in a tight, strained voice, slapping the grimy, battered bonnet. 'Or did you have to buy it?'

'It's mine,' Leonidas answered, taking a breath from quenching his thirst and watching her from under the thickness of his dark lashes.

'Perhaps it's time you bought a new one,' she suggested cheekily, amused, deciding that it wasn't only the tyre that needed changing. The bodywork looked as if it wouldn't object to a lick of fresh paint either.

'Perhaps it's time you stopped having a laugh at my expense.'

Was that what she was doing? 'I'm sorry.' Seeing his eyes darkening, quickly Kayla strove to suppress her mocking banter. After all, he probably couldn't afford anything better, she thought. Not like Craig, with his company Jaguar and his inflated expense account. This man would have no such perks. 'I didn't mean to laugh about it— honest.'

'Didn't you?' He had emptied his glass with one final long draught. Setting it aside, he came to where Kayla stood with her hand resting on the top of the radiator grid, as though in apology to the vehicle itself. 'I suppose you measure a man's status by the type of car he drives, huh?'

'No.'

'What would you prefer? A Porsche? Or a Mercedes?' he asked roughly.

'Well, both would be nice…' Her voice tailed off when she noticed how forbidding he looked, and she realised that she wasn't just imagining that hardening in his voice. 'I wasn't making fun of you. Not really,' she tagged on, suddenly afraid that he might think less of her if he thought she had been. 'I suppose I was just getting my own back.'

'For what?'

'For embarrassing me earlier. Making me feel awkward. When you said I was being too inquisitive about your private life.'

He laughed very softly then, his strong implacable features suddenly losing some of their austerity. His eyes, however, were disturbingly reflective as they rested on her face.

'And I thought you were doing it just to prompt some reaction from me,' he murmured silkily, with no apology for silencing her earlier.

'Prompt some reaction from you?' Kayla's throat contracted with heightening sexual tension. 'Why would I want to do that?'

'Because I'm probably one of the only men you've met who isn't instantly falling over himself to respond to your temptingly sexy signals.'

'I'm not giving off *any* signals!' Kayla breathed, mortified. 'And I'm certainly not trying to get your attention.'

'Aren't you?' Those shrewd eyes tugged over her flushed, indignant features, regarding, assessing and stripping her of her deepest and hottest secrets. 'You wouldn't have come out here looking like this...' an all-encompassing glance took in breasts thrust tantalisingly upwards by the shaping of the cups and skimpy briefs barely skimming her abdomen '…if you weren't.'

Shamefully, she wished she had bothered to retrieve her cover-up before flaunting herself in front of him like this. Because that *was* what she had been doing, she admitted silently. Flaunting herself.

She wanted to say something to redeem herself. Or simply to run away. Anything but stay there and face him like this.

She wished she had run when he suddenly reached up and cupped her cheek, his broad thumb playing across the softness of her pouting lips.

'If I made love to you, Kayla,' he said huskily, 'it would be a fleeting moment's pleasure. That's all. No commitment. No strings. And I don't think you came here to let some man with his own issues to sort out use you like that. A girl like you needs something more than anything I could offer you. Something more meaningful. Not a brief fling to try and forget the man who cheated on you with a few hours of what I can't deny would be sensational pleasure.'

He was deadly serious, but even his words were exciting her. Or was it his thumb, tracing the curve of her plump lower lip, forcing her to close her eyes against the reckless desire to taste him? To inhale his musky animal scent mingling with the smell of grease and metal and everything that made this man exciting to her?

'Who said I want you to make love to me?' she murmured in pointless protest, her eyes inky beneath lashes still half-lowered against his gaze.

'You're inviting it with every denial you utter,' he breathed hoarsely, his voice overlaid with desire. 'And you're not so naïve as not to realise that you're making me as hard as a rock.'

'You're wrong!' she argued breathlessly, and in the only way she knew of saving face she pulled away from him, almost tripping over her own feet in her flip-flops as she virtually ran back to the house.

Upstairs, away from Philomena's shrewd eyes, she went into the shower-room and peeled off the bikini that seemed to be sticking to her.

Why on earth was she so attracted to him? she berated herself under the cool jets of the shower, trying to lather away the sensual heat from her body and that elusive scent of him that still clung to her skin where he had briefly touched her.

He had admitted himself that he was a man with issues.

Woman issues! Which was why he had shut her up, coming back from the beach today.

Well, what did she care? His business was his business. As far as she was concerned, he was simply a man who had helped her out of a difficult situation. Nothing more. It was just that she couldn't seem to stop making a fool of herself when she was with him, let alone concentrate on anything but him when she wasn't!

She tried to think about the past couple of months. Her ex. What had driven her here. Tried to stir up some other emotions to blot out the crazy, reckless feelings she was experiencing for Leon.

But, try though she did, feeling bitter suddenly seemed like a wasted emotion—because Craig and what he had done didn't seem to matter so much any more.

CHAPTER SIX

KAYLA DIDN'T SEE Leon the next day, or the day after that, and when he did come down to the cottage again, looking stupendous in a white T-shirt and light, hip-hugging trousers, it was only to deliver logs to Philomena.

'So you're still roadworthy, then?' Kayla remarked, almost coyly, when he came into the sitting room after offloading and stacking the logs beside the huge indoor oven, still embarrassingly mindful of their conversation the last time they had met.

'Just about,' Leonidas reassured her with a self-effacing grimace. 'And I see that you're just about as cheeky as ever.'

'No, I'm not,' Kayla asserted, thrilled nevertheless by the sensual gleam in those midnight-black eyes that seemed to promise some delightful retribution if she didn't stop. Wildly she wondered if he had been right the other day, and she *had* been taunting him solely for his attention. Because despite all he had said about no attachments and no strings, she wanted that attention now—like crazy! 'We were wondering why we hadn't seen you,' she said, as nonchalantly as she could.

'We?' He picked up on her deliberate choice of pronoun—and on the little tremor she couldn't keep out of her voice. Obviously, from the way his mouth compressed in mild amusement. 'Are you saying you missed me?'

'No.' Kayla was glad that Philomena had left the room—though not before she'd noticed how the woman had laid a grateful hand on Leon's arm for the work he had just done. The unspoken affection the two of them shared touched Kayla immensely.

Yet she *had* missed him, she thought, and Leon knew it too—evidently from the way he laughed in response.

'In that case you won't object to spending the day with me,' he said, deliberately misinterpreting what she had said. 'Philomena told me you were asking one of her neighbours about the little island the other day—about if you could book a trip across there.'

He meant that dark mass of land she could see jutting out of the sea from practically every aspect of this hillside.

'She also mentioned that you spend far too much time worrying that you aren't doing enough to help her around the place. She wants you to enjoy your holiday—so do I—and as there are no organised trips to that island I'll be happy to take you over there myself.'

Even as he was suggesting it Leonidas told himself that he was being unwise. He had assured Kayla—as well as himself—that he wasn't prepared to have any sort of relationship with her, but try as he might he just couldn't keep away. Yet if he spent time with her, he warned himself, he would be deceiving her with every word he uttered. And if he didn't…?

If he didn't then he'd go mad thinking about her, he admitted silently, feeling the thrust of his scorching libido flaring into life just from sparring with her, not to mention from the scent of her, which was acting on his senses as powerfully as if he'd just opened the door on some willing wanton's boudoir.

Her appearance wasn't helping his control. She was wearing white shorts, which showed off far too much of those deliciously creamy legs, and a sleeveless lemon blouse tied under her breasts. It revealed just enough of her shallow cleavage to make him want to see more, and left her gradually tanning slender midriff delightfully bare.

'Thanks, but I think I'll give it a miss today,' she said, disappointing him.

'Suit yourself,' he muttered, turning away. He was relieved that the decision had been made—especially since he had been entertaining the strongest desire to tug open that tantalising little blouse and mould her sensitive breasts to his palms until she sobbed with the pleasure.

'Well...'

Her sudden hesitancy stopped him in his tracks. Battling to control his raging anatomy, he didn't turn around, his breath locking in his lungs as he heard her tentative little suggestion behind him.

'If you could just give me a minute...?'

He swung round then, his desire veiled by his immense powers of self-control. His eyes, as they clashed with hers, were smouldering with a dark intensity and he saw an answering response in the darkening blue of hers that was as hungry as it was guarded.

Almost cleverly guarded, he thought, but not quite enough. She was as on fire for him as he was for her, he recognised, regardless of any feelings she might still be harbouring over that louse who had let her down.

Kayla, as she stood there, captured by the powerful hold of his gaze, felt a skein of excitement unravelling inside her and knew that a watershed had been reached. That with one look and one inconsequential unfinished sentence a silent understanding had somehow passed between them. She had crossed a bridge that was already burning behind her and she knew there could be no turning back.

'No rowing boat today?' Kayla remarked, surprised when, after driving them to a beach further along the coast, Leon guided her towards a small motor boat moored alongside a wooden jetty. 'I didn't think you'd be seen dead in anything less than fifty years old!' she said laughingly.

'Didn't you?' he drawled, with a challenging and deliciously sensual gleam in his eyes as he handed her into the boat. 'Contrary to your thinking, *hrisi mou,* I can...' he hesitated, thinking of the words '...come good when circumstances demand.'

'And *do* circumstances demand?' she enquired

airily, in spite of her pulse, which was racing from his nearness and his softly spoken endearment.

'Oh, yes,' he breathed with barely veiled meaning. 'I think they do.'

It was a day of delight and surprises.

With effortless dexterity Leonidas steered the boat through the sparkling blue water, following the rocky coast of his own island to begin with, and pointing out coves and deserted beaches only accessible from the sea.

Having a field-day with her camera, Kayla lapped up the magic of her surroundings whilst using every opportunity to grab secretive and not so secretive shots of this dynamic man she was with: at the wheel, in profile, with his brow furrowed in concentration, or turning to talk to her with that sexy, sidelong pull of his mouth that never failed to do funny things to her stomach. She captured him looking out over the dark body of water they were cutting through, his T-shirt pulled taut across his broad muscular back, his black hair as windswept as hers from the exhilarating speed at which they were travelling.

She'd need to remember, she realised almost desperately, wondering why it was so important to her to capture everything about this holiday. This island. These precious few hours. This man.

Suddenly aware, he glanced over his shoulder and, easing back on the throttle, said challengingly, 'Don't you think you've taken enough?' She was about to make some quip about it being her 'fix', but he cut across her before she could with, 'What are you going to do? Put them on the internet?'

With a questioning look at him, not sure how to take what he'd said, she pretended to be considering it, and with a half-tantalising, half-nervous little giggle, answered, 'I might.'

'You do that and our association ends right now.' His contesting tone and manner caused her to flinch.

'If you're that concerned, then keep it,' she invited, holding the camera out to him. She hadn't forgotten what a private person he was. 'I promise I'm not going to publish them on the web, but take it if you don't trust me not to.'

For a moment her candour made Leonidas hold back. How could he demand or even expect integrity from her when he wasn't being straight himself?

Briefly he felt like flinging caution to the winds

and telling her the truth. Only the thought of the repercussions that could follow stopped him.

She would be angry, that was certain. But he had come here seeking respite from all the glamour and superficiality that went hand in hand with who he really was, and he wasn't ready yet to relinquish his precious anonymity. It didn't help reminding himself that it was primarily because of trusting a woman that he had felt driven to take some time out. Because of being too careless and believing that a casual but willing bed partner would share the same ethics as he.

Not that this girl was in any way like the mercenary vamp with whom he had unwisely shared the weekend that had proved so costly to his pride and reputation. But his billionaire status and lifestyle still generated interest, despite his best attempts to keep it low-key—and never more so since his unfortunate affair with the media-hungry Esmeralda—and Kayla was only human after all. What a boost it would be to her bruised ego after being ditched so cruelly by her fiancé for news of her liaison with a man whose corporate achievements weren't entirely unknown to filter back to the world press. One text home to this Lorna might be all it would take to bring the paparazzi here in their droves.

'It's stolen enough of your time from me for one day,' he said, smiling. Yet he still took the camera she was offering and stowed it away in a recess beneath the wheel.

They had lunch on the boat—a feast of lobster and cheeses, fresh bread and a blend of freshly squeezed juice. Afterwards there were delicate pastries filled with fruit and walnuts, and others creamy with the tangy freshness of lime.

Kayla savoured it all as she'd never savoured a meal before, and there was wonder mixed in with her appreciation.

'This must have set you back a fortune,' she couldn't help remarking when she had finished.

'Let me worry about that,' he told her unassumingly.

'But to hire a boat like this doesn't come cheap...' Even if only for a day, she thought. 'And as for that lunch...' She wondered if he would have eaten as well had he been alone and decided that he wouldn't, guessing that he must have been counting on her being unable to resist coming with him today.

'What are you concerned about, Kayla?' he asked

softly, closing the cool box that had contained their picnic before stowing it away. 'That I might have spent more than you think I can justifiably afford? Or is it finding yourself in my debt that's making you uneasy?'

'A bit of both, I suppose,' she admitted truthfully. After all, she'd always been used to paying her way when she was with a man, to never taking more out of a relationship than she was prepared to put in. Emotionally as well as financially, she thought with a little stab of self-derision as she remembered how with Craig she had wound up giving everything and receiving nothing, coming out a first-rate fool in the end.

'Don't worry about it,' Leonidas advised. 'I promise you I'm not likely to starve for the rest of my holiday. As for the boat, I hired it to take myself off exploring today. Your coming with me is just a bonus, so there's no need to feel awkward or indebted in any way. If you want to contribute something, then your enjoyment will suffice,' he assured her, and refrained from adding that most women he'd known would have taken his generosity as their due.

The island, when they came ashore, was beautiful. Lonely and uninhabited, it was merely a haven for wildlife, with only numerous birds and insects making their voices heard above the warm wind and the wash of the sea in the cove where they had left the boat.

There was no distinct path, and the climb through the surprisingly green vegetation was hot and steep, but the feeling of freedom at the top was worth a thousand climbs.

It was like standing in their own uninhabited world. In every direction the deep blue of the sky met the deeper blue of the sea. Looking back across the distance they had covered, Kayla saw the hulk of mountainous land they had left with its forests and its craggy coastline slumbering in a haze of heat.

There were huge stones amongst the grass— sculpted stones of an ancient ruin, overgrown with scrub and wild flowers, a sad and silent testimony to the beliefs of some long-lost civilisation.

'You said you came to sort out some issues?' Kayla reminded him, venturing to broach what she had been dying to ask him since they had left that morning. 'What sort of issues?' she pressed, look-ing seawards at the waves creaming onto a distant beach and wondering if it was the one where she had first seen him over a week ago. 'Woman issues?' she enquired, more tentatively now.

He was standing with his foot on one of the stones that had once formed part of the ancient temple, with one hand resting on his knee. The wind was lifting his hair, sweeping it back off features suddenly so uncompromising that he looked like a marauding mythical god, surveying all he intended to conquer.

'Among other things,' he said, but he didn't enlarge on the women in his life or tell her what those 'other things' were.

Kayla moved away from him, pulling a brightly flowering weed from a crack in what had formed part of a wall. She was getting used to his uncommunicative ways.

She was surprised, therefore, when he suddenly said, 'I used to dream of owning this island when I was a boy. I used to sit on that hillside...' he pointed to a distant spot across the water, indiscernible through the heat haze '...and imagine all I was going to do with it. The big house. The swimming pool. The riding stables.'

'And dogs?' Kayla inserted, her eyes gleaming, following him into a make-believe world of her own.

'Yes, lots of dogs.'

So he liked animals, she realised, deriving warm pleasure from the knowledge. Contrarily, though, she wrinkled her nose. 'Too costly to feed.' Laughingly she pretended to discount that idea. 'And too much heartache if they get sick or run away.'

'They couldn't run away,' Leonidas reminded her. 'Not unless they were proficient swimmers.'

'Haven't you ever heard of the doggy paddle?' She giggled, enjoying playing this little game with him. Her eyes were bright and her cheeks were glowing from an exhilaration that had nothing to do with their climb. 'So you were going to build a house with a swimming pool? And have horses? Racehorses, of course.'

He shot her a sceptical glance. 'Now you're wandering into the realms of fantasy,' he chided, amused.

'Well, if you can own the island and have a house with lots of dogs, I can have racehorses,' Kayla insisted light-heartedly.

'They'd fall off the edge before they'd covered a mile,' he commented dryly. 'I was talking about what seemed totally realistic to a twelve-year-old boy.'

Tugging her windswept hair out of her eyes, Kayla pulled a face. 'But then you grew up?'

'Yes,' he said heavily. 'I grew up.' And all he had wanted to do was run as far away from these islands and everything he had called home as he could possibly get.

'What happened?' Kayla asked, frowning. She couldn't help but notice the tension clenching his mouth and the hard line of his jaw.

'My mother died when I was fourteen, then my grandfather shortly afterwards. My father and I didn't see eye to eye,' he enlightened her.

'Why not?'

'Why do we not get on with some people and yet gel so perfectly with others? Especially those who are supposed to be closest to us?' He shrugged, his strong features softening a little. 'Differing opinions? A clash of personalities? Maybe even because we are too much alike. Why aren't *you* close to your mother?' he outlined as an example.

Watching a lizard dart along the jagged edge of the wall and disappear over the side, Kayla considered his question. 'I suppose all those things,' she admitted, rather ruefully. And then, keen to shrug off the serious turn the conversation had taken, she said, 'So, are you going to sketch me a picture of this house?'

'No.'

'Why not?' She had seen him scribbling in his notepad again, when he had been waiting for her in the truck outside Philomena's, and wondered what he could possibly have been doing if he *hadn't* been sketching. He'd also been speaking to somebody on his cell phone at the same time, Kayla remembered, but had cut the call short, leaning across to open the passenger door for her when he had seen her coming. She'd wondered if he'd been speaking to a woman and, if he had, whether it was the woman at the heart of his 'issues'.

'It isn't what I do,' Leonidas said.

'No son of mine is going to disgrace the Vassalio name by painting for a living!'

Leonidas could still hear his father's bellowing as he ridiculed his talent, his love of perspective and light and colour, beating it out of him—sometimes literally—as he destroyed the results of his teenage son's labours and with them all the creativity in his soul. Art was a feeling and feelings were weakness, his father had drummed into him. And no Vassalio male had ever been weak.

So he had channelled his driving energies into

creating new worlds out of blocks of clay and concrete, in innovative designs that had leaped off the paper and formed the basis of his own developments. Developments that had made him rich beyond his wildest dreams. And with the money it had all come tumbling into his lap. Influence. Respect. Women. So many women that he could have had his pick of any of them. Yet he hadn't found one who was more disposed to him personally than she was to the state of his bank balance. Not beyond the pleasures of the bedroom at any rate, he thought with a self-deprecating mental grimace. In that it seemed he was never able to fail.

'So what about you, Kayla? Didn't you have any aspirations?'

'I suppose I did but not like yours,' she said, twirling the stalk of a pink flower in her fingers. 'I think I was always practical and realistic. Besides, I was brought up with the understanding that if you don't expect you can't be disappointed.'

'And because of that you never allowed yourself to dream?'

He was sitting on one of the larger stones, one leg bent, the other stretched out in front of him, and Kayla tried to avoid noticing how the cloth of his trousers pulled tautly over one muscular thigh.

'Of course I did,' she uttered, wondering why she suddenly felt as if she needed to defend herself. 'But I've never been one for mooning over things I can't have. Especially things which are totally out of my reach.'

He leaned back and crossed his arms, his muscles bunching, emphasising their latent strength. 'And you don't believe that everything is within your reach if you jump high enough?'

He made it sound almost credible, which seemed quite out of kilter, Kayla thought, with his laid-back attitude to life.

'If you jump too high you usually fall flat on your face. Anyway, you're one to talk,' she commented, still hurt over his refusal to give her a glimpse into even the smallest area of his life. 'You don't even have a steady job.'

'I get by.'

'But nothing that offers real security or fulfils your potential?'

'And why is it so important to fulfil my "potential"?' he quoted. His eyes were dark and inscrutable, giving nothing of his thoughts away.

'Because everybody needs a purpose. Some sort of goal in life,' Kayla stressed.

'And what is your goal, *glykia mou?*'

The sensuality with which he spoke suddenly seemed to emphasise the isolation of their surroundings, and with it the fundamental objective of each other's existence.

'To be happy.'

'And that's it? Just to be happy?' He looked both surprised and mildly amused. 'And how do you propose to achieve this happiness?'

Cynicism had replaced the mocking amusement of a moment ago. She could see it in the curling of his firm, rather cruel-looking mouth—a mouth she was aching to feel covering hers again.

'By staying grounded and true to myself, and not ever attempting to be something I'm not,' she uttered—croakily, because of where her thoughts had taken her. Afraid that she was in danger of sounding a little bit self-righteous, she added, 'By appreciating nature. Things like this.' She cast a glance around her at the wilderness of the island. At everything that was timeless. Untrammelled and free. 'By creating a happy home. Having children one day. And animals. Lots of animals.'

'And that's all it's going to take?' Again he looked marginally surprised. 'Setting up home and having babies?'

'It's better than being a drifter,' she remarked,

knowing she was overstepping the mark yet unable to stop herself, 'without any ambition whatsoever.'

'You think I don't have ambition?'

'Well, *do* you?' she challenged, aware that she had no right to, as she pulled her hair out of her eyes again, yet driven by the feeling that he was mocking her values and finding them wanting.

'You'd be surprised. But just for argument's sake, what do you see me doing?' How would *you* have me realise this ambition?'

'You're good with cars,' Kayla remarked, ignoring the mockery infiltrating his question. 'You could be a mechanic. You could even start your own business. With the prices they charge for servicing and repairs these days you could make a comfortable living.'

'If I were a mechanic I wouldn't be able to take time off to come to places like this for weeks at a time.' His mouth compressed in exasperating dismissal. 'And I certainly wouldn't have met you.'

It was there in his eyes—raw, pure hunger. The same hunger that had been eating away at her ever since they had met and which now was taking every ounce of her will-power not to acknowledge.

'You could save enough to be able to buy your own garage,' she went on in a huskier voice. 'Put a manager in. Then you could take time off once in a while.'

'You think it's that simple? A steady job? A mortgage on a business and—hey! You're rich! That isn't how it works, Kayla.'

'How do you know if you don't try? Anyway, it was only a suggestion,' she reminded him, noticing how snugly his T-shirt moulded itself to the contours of his chest, the way his whole body seemed to pulse with unimpeded virility. 'You have to have drive and determination too.'

He laughed. 'And in that you think I'm sadly lacking?'

'You said that, not me,' she reminded him sombrely. 'I was only trying to help.'

'For which I'm very grateful,' he said, with that familiar mocking curl to his lips. 'But that sort of help I'm really able to do without.'

'Suit yourself,' she uttered, moving away from the ruin and gasping at the speed with which he leaped up and joined her as she came onto a plain of shorter grasses, interspersed with tall ferns and flowering shrubs.

'And now you're looking and feeling thoroughly chastened,' he remarked laughingly, catching her hand in his while his fervid gaze played with dark intensity over her small fine features, coming to rest on the pouting fullness of her mouth.

'You're very perceptive,' she breathed, hardly able to speak because of the wild responses leaping through her from his dangerous and electrifying nearness. 'And for a man without ambition you certainly believe in getting what you want.'

'You'd better believe it,' he asserted softly.

Even in a whisper his voice conveyed a determination of purpose that none of the self-important types she had known had ever possessed, and it sent little skeins of excitement unravelling through Kayla's insides.

'As for my lack of ambition... As I said, you'd be surprised. But what might *not* surprise you right now is to know that my most burning ambition is to feel you lying beneath me and to taste those sweet lips again, *agape mou*. To make love to you slowly and thoroughly until you're crying out for my length inside you. And I think at this moment you want the same thing—regardless of how unfulfilled or goalless you think I am.'

She wanted to protest but it would have been pointless, Kayla realised. She was already melting the moment his mouth came down over hers. She responded to it hungrily—greedily—her arms going around his neck, pulling him down to her as if she could never have enough.

Their kissing was hot and impassioned—a passion demanding only to be fed as, mouths fused, they sank together onto the sun-warmed grass. And Leonidas did as he'd wanted to do since he had arrived at Philomena's house that morning: tugged firmly on the ties of Kayla's blouse.

He gave a sigh of satisfaction when it fell open, revealing the pale lace and satin of her bra.

Slipping a finger inside, he revelled in the warmth of her soft skin before he pulled down the lace, releasing one modest-sized breast from its restraining cup.

Small, he measured, moulding the soft pale mound to his work-roughened palm, yet perfectly in proportion to the rest of her and more than satisfyingly sensitive, he realised as he caressed the pale pink areola into burgeoning arousal.

She moaned softly from the excitement of what he was doing to her. She arched her back, aching for his mouth over the swollen nipple, and almost hit the roof when he suddenly dipped his head and granted her wish.

There was no one and nothing around them. Nothing except the wash of the waves on the beach below them and the wind that was teasing her hair into the finest strands of spun gold, inviting him to touch it, caress it, lose himself in the perfume that was all woman, all her own.

His lips were burning kisses over her breasts, her throat, the tender line of her jaw, finding and capturing her mouth again with the dominant pressure of his.

'Leon...'

She breathed his name into his mouth, saying it as no one had said it in a long, long time. No one called him Leon these days. Only Philomena...

Far away from this idyll, back in London, in Athens and on the corporate world stage, he was known only as Leonidas. Leonidas Vassalio. Hard-headed businessman. Decisive. Practical. Ruthless...

The reminder almost dragged him back to his senses, but not quite.

Her hands had ripped open his shirt, and he gave a deep guttural groan at their caressing warmth over his bared chest, but they were travelling downwards—down and down—in a quest to drive him wild, break his control.

He sucked in his breath, every nerve flexing like tautened wire, until finally, when she touched that most intimate part of him, even through his clothes, he was lost.

He wanted to stop this madness. Come clean about who he was. Because how could he justifiably do this with her if he didn't?

But as if sensing his reticent moment she was begging him not to stop, and her whimpers of need were all it took to bring about his final undoing.

If he told her who he was now he would be inviting her anger, and he couldn't face that, he realised in meagre justification. Couldn't ruin the mood and her artless belief in him no matter how much he knew he should.

It took little effort to remove her shorts, with her lace-edged briefs following them to where he'd cast them aside.

She was beautiful. A natural blonde, he noted with a soft smile of satisfaction as her legs parted before him and she lifted her body in a sobbing invitation for him to claim his prize.

It would be so easy, Leonidas thought, to remove his own clothes and take all that she was offering, assuage the fire that was burning in his groin. Just one thrust could take him to paradise…

He was hotter and harder than he had ever been in his life just from thinking about such damning pleasure, but through the torment of his stimulating thoughts a shred of sanity—of principle—remained.

He couldn't do it. Couldn't abuse her trust like that. Not while he still felt it necessary to deceive her. And yet she was slick with wanting, sobbing her need and her craving for release from this passion he had aroused.

She was lying with her face turned to one side and her arms above her head in a gesture of pure surrender. An angel, he thought, inviting him to share heaven with her. Or Eve, tempting him among the grasses of her sensuous Eden.

With torturous restraint he dipped his head and pressed his lips to the heated satin of her pulsing ribcage, his mouth moving with calculated precision over her slender waist to the flat plane of her abdomen and beyond. Very gently he parted her legs wider and slipped his arms beneath her splayed thighs.

Feeling his mouth against that most intimate part of her drew a shuddering gasp from Kayla. That dark hair brushing the sensitive flesh of her inner thigh was a stimulation she couldn't even have imagined.

It was the most erotic experience of her life. She

had been intimate with a man before, but it had never felt like this. This abandoning of herself so completely to a pleasure that promised to drive her wild.

He knew just how to tease and titillate, just where and how to touch, employing his lips and the heat of his tongue to start a fire building in her as he tasted the honeyed sweetness of her body.

She thought she would die from the pleasure of it, and her body tautened in breathless expectation as flames of sensation licked along her nerve-endings and produced a burning tingle along her thighs.

Her juices flowed from her body, mingling with the moistness of his, anointing his roughened jaw with everything she was—until the mind-blowing sensation proved too much and she cried out as the fire consumed her in an orgasm of pulsating, interminable throbs.

Her sensitivity increased until she couldn't take any more pleasure, and she clamped her thighs around him, trapping him there, holding him to her in a sobbing ecstatic agony of release until the last embers of the fire he had ignited finally died away.

After a while, Kayla looked up at him where he lay beside her, propped up on an elbow. 'Why didn't you...?' Crazily, even after the intimacy they had shared she was too embarrassed to say it.

'Why didn't I what?' Leonidas leaned across her, tracing the curve of her cheek before picking a small windblown flower out of her hair. 'Take what I wanted?' he supplied, helping her.

She nodded, closing her eyes against the exquisite tenderness of his touch.

'Because I don't think you're a girl who indulges in casual sex, and you wouldn't have thanked me for it tomorrow.'

'Because you think I'm on the rebound?' Suddenly self-conscious of her nakedness, when he hadn't even undressed beyond his gaping shirt, she sat up to retrieve her clothes. 'I'm not—I promise you,' she said resolutely, wriggling into her panties.

She was well and truly over Craig now. But perhaps there were other reasons for Leon not taking their lovemaking the whole way. Perhaps he was remaining faithful to someone, she thought uneasily. Someone who moved him to anger and roused his passions in a way she might never be able to do...

'Did you bring *her* here?' She couldn't look at him as she started fastening her blouse.

'Who?'

'The woman you won't talk about?' she said grievously.

He laughed—a deep, warm sound on the scented air, mingling with the drone of insects and the mellifluous birdsong. 'You really are a very imaginative little lady.'

'Not as imaginative as you, with your island mansion and your racehorses,' she accused, kneeling up to tug her shorts on.

'Uh-uh,' he denied. 'The racehorses were your idea,' he reminded her with a hint of humour in his eyes, although the slashes of colour across his cheeks were evidence of the passion that still rode him. 'And now I really think it's time that we started back.'

'I'm being serious,' she stressed, wishing he wouldn't continue to evade the issue, wondering if he was only doing it because there really was someone else.

'So am I,' he breathed heavily, getting up and pulling her with him, and this time his determination brooked no resistance.

CHAPTER SEVEN

LOOKING BACK, LEONIDAS wasn't sure how he had managed to stop himself making love to Kayla that afternoon. Heaven knew he had wanted to. A fact not made any easier by the knowledge of how much she had wanted him, too. But there were ethics to be observed, and there was no way that he could have taken all she had been offering when he wasn't being straight with her. It had all boiled down to guilt, he decided shamefully. Guilt because he wasn't telling her the truth.

But the truth was that he had come here to be alone. Not to indulge in any social or sexual entanglements with a girl who could carry him along with her ridiculous yet infectious sense of make-believe. Well, make-believe to *her,* at any rate. Because he could afford that island, had it been for sale—and a dozen like it, did she but know it. But it seemed like a lifetime since he had indulged in that childish game, and he had found it oddly refreshing.

In the world he moved in there was no room for fantasising or dreaming. Only for cold hard facts and figures. Securing deals. That was living the dream. Or so he had thought.

Until now, though, he hadn't begun to realise how deeply and for how long his dreams had been buried. Firstly by his father, and then more recently beneath the weight of his own responsibilities. He had been so busy making money—reaping the benefits of all he had worked for during the past decade or more—that he hadn't taken the time even to question where those dreams had gone. And now this little nobody had come along, making him question his values. He was annoyed with himself for allowing her to get under his skin to such a degree. But that didn't change the fact that he wanted her more than he had wanted any woman in a long time—much less one who would have been in her own marriage bed right now if things had worked out as they should have.

A hard possessiveness kicked in as he imagined her naked with the faceless, double-crossing character who had betrayed her—he could only temper his indignation at the thought of the two of them together by imagining himself in Kayla's bed. And that brought other problems as his body hardened in response to imagining her sobs of pure pleasure directed at him and him alone as he made himself master of her body.

But things couldn't go on as they were. He was either going to have to come clean at some stage, he decided grimly, or end their relationship before it went any further. Neither prospect filled him with any pleasure.

He knew exactly what she thought about company men, and after the experience she had had with that lowest of the low fiancé of hers—not to mention her father—she'd be blameless for thinking he was no better. Yet staying away from her wasn't an option he welcomed either. He was just relieved that his secretary had e-mailed him with some plans that needed his urgent attention, so that for today at least he didn't have to think about how he could come clean with Kayla. However he chose to tell her, he knew she wasn't going to welcome finding out...

When Leon didn't put in an appearance that day, and didn't come down the next morning, Kayla jumped at Philomena's suggestion that she drive up to the farmhouse with some bread Philomena had just baked.

She'd scarcely given a thought to her ex since Leon had taken her over to that island, she realised, noticing how it seemed to shimmer in the morning sun. She couldn't help marvelling at the difference between the two men and wondering what she had ever seen in Craig.

Had her love for him been so shallow that the first man who came along could make her forget him and the hurt he had caused her so completely? But then Leon wasn't just any man, she reminded herself, with a sudden tightening of her breasts and that familiar stirring of heat at the very heart of her femininity. He made her feel like no other man had ever made her feel.

A throbbing excitement leaped along her veins at the memory of their afternoon on that islet, when he had driven her crazy for him, playing with her like a love-toy, winding her up only to let her run wild with delirious sensation as he had taken her to heights her mental and physical being had never scaled before.

She had wanted him so much! And it had been patently obvious that he wanted her. So why hadn't he taken their lovemaking to its ultimate conclusion? Was it because there was someone else? But he had called her imaginative when she had broached the subject with him, so perhaps it was simply that he didn't think she was ready to embark on a relationship with him—in which case, she decided with a delicious little shiver, it was up to her to show him that she was.

When she arrived at the farmhouse her heart gave a little leap when she saw the truck parked outside.

So he was in! She wondered if she was being too presumptuous in coming. Supposing he didn't want to see her? Or she'd disappointed him in some way?

Feeling queasy in the stomach just from entertaining that possibility, she tripped lightly round to the glass-paned peeling doors at the back of the house. One creaked open at her less than confident knock.

When she called out there was no reply, and so gingerly she moved inside, still calling his name. He wasn't in the sitting room, and nor did he emerge from the kitchen when she moved enquiringly towards it.

Perhaps he'd gone for a walk, she mused, standing there in the hall, wondering what to do.

About to take a look outside, she heard a sudden thud on the boarded floor above. She dumped her carrier bag with the bread she'd brought on an old pine chest just inside the door.

'Leon?' she called out, and when there was still no response, unthinkingly she raced up the stairs.

His bedroom was in shadow, with semi-closed shutters, but a quick glance towards the bed revealed him lying there on his back, still drugged from sleep, groping blindly for something on the floor on the other side of the bed.

Kayla moved over and, picking up a chunky little clock, replaced it on the cabinet beside the bedside lamp.

'Are you all right?' she asked, knowing what an early bird he usually was. It was already after ten and she'd obviously woken him, she realised, guessing he'd reached for the clock and knocked it over when he'd heard her calling him.

'I must have crashed out,' he mumbled, drawing an arm across his forehead. His eyes were heavy with sleep and his hair was dishevelled and, like his unshaven jaw, satanically dark. 'What are you doing here?'

'I brought you some bread. I thought you were out, but the door was open,' Kayla responded with a nervous gesture of her hand. She was aware that she was gabbling, but it was difficult to do anything else when faced with the sight of his bronzed body, naked save for the fine sheet that barely covered his hips and certainly left nothing to the imagination. 'Aren't you pleased to see me?'

'What do you think?' he drawled, in a voice thickened by sleep and by the involuntary response of his anatomy.

Heated colour touched Kayla's cheeks and yet she couldn't keep her gaze from straying to his potent virility. Driven by something more powerful than her own reasoning, she dropped down onto the bed.

'I think you must be overjoyed,' she whispered, touching kisses to the warm, undulating muscles of his chest, using the pale, sensuous fountain of her hair to caress him as her lips moved over the tautened flesh of his tight lean waist and her hands dealt tremblingly with the sheet.

He let out a deep shuddering gasp of anticipation. 'Why did you come?' he asked heavily.

'I just thought that one good turn deserved another,' Kayla whispered, feathering kisses over his tightly muscled abdomen. She didn't know where she was finding the courage to seduce him like this. She only knew by instinct alone that he was a man who liked his women confident and worldly, not wimpish and nursing the old wounds of a previous relationship.

'Close your eyes,' she ordered softly, getting up.

Leonidas's heart seemed to stop, and then thundered into life when she came back to the bed and straddled him. She was wearing a white top with a little red skirt that swirled about her thighs, and his mind whirled in a vortex of conflicting thoughts as he realised that she had obviously removed what she had been wearing underneath.

'Kayla. Stop this…' He wasn't sure whether he'd spoken the words or whether they were just buzzing feverishly through his brain.

'Why? Is it too early for you?' Kayla teased, excitement driving her even as her mind raced with interminable doubts.

Was she carrying things too far? Didn't he like a woman taking the initiative? He was more down to earth and unfettered by convention than any man she had ever met. He didn't want a woman who was anything but what *he* was. Not someone weighed down with emotional baggage; someone who didn't know her own mind.

Beneath her Leonidas shivered as he felt her sliding down his body, the moist heat of her searing his skin like a molten poultice.

'Dear—!' He swallowed the profanity, his breathing laboured, his body on fire. He had to stop this! But as her soft mouth took possession of him his senses spun into chaos.

He had never felt so powerless, and yet at the same time so shamelessly empowered. His body was a temple of pleasure at which this amazing woman was worshipping.

He felt his size increase and harden like burning, quivering steel. His body was taut as a bow, holding back the flaming arrow it needed to release before it consumed him in its raging inferno.

He fought to contain it, the struggle almost overwhelming him. And just when he thought he had won the battle she slid along his length, positioning herself above him to take him into her.

He tried to pull back, but he was powerless to do anything but push against her slick hot wetness, groaning in defeat as he allowed himself the freedom to let her do whatever she would.

Looking down at him, Kayla registered the rapturous agony on his face, that line of pained pleasure between his closed lids. It lent him a vulnerability she hadn't seen before—one that called to everything in her that was soft and feminine and tender—and yet she felt powerful too. She was in control and glorying in it, dominating the pace and the depth and the rhythm. That was until she heard the guttural masculine groan when he suddenly clamped his hands over her hips and pushed harder and more determinedly into her.

The depth of penetration dragged a small cry of ecstasy from her lips. She felt the explosion of his seed deep within her and started to climax almost instantaneously.

It was the most fulfilling experience of her life.

They were both breathing heavily when she collapsed, wet and gasping, against the warm damp cushion of his chest, and then he was rolling her round so that she was lying pressed close to his side.

'What was all that about?' he quizzed, as soon as he could speak again. His breathing was still heavy and laboured.

Kayla wasn't sure whether there was disapproval in his husky tones. 'Didn't you like it?' she enquired, almost diffidently.

'Of *course* I liked it!' he shot back, his voice incredulous. 'But right now I'm not sure whether to applaud you for your resourcefulness or to paddle that pretty bare bottom of yours and send you packing back to Philomena's.'

'Why?' An uneasy line pleated Kayla's brows as she lay facing him with her hair wildly dishevelled. 'Do Greek men always have to be the dominant partner?' She was beginning to feel hurt and embarrassed.

'No. But whoever chooses to be should take responsibility for what they're doing. Is there any chance that you could be pregnant after that delightful little escapade?'

'Of course not! I'm not that stupid!' she snapped, trying to sit up and failing when he kept her anchored to his side. She didn't feel it was necessary to add that she was taking the pill. She had tried to come off it after her break-up with Craig, but her periods had gone so haywire that her doctor had suggested it might be best for her to keep taking it until her emotions were on a more even keel.

'So what happens now?' Leonidas asked, his breath seeming to shiver through his lungs.

'What do you mean?' Blue eyes searched the midnight-darkness of his for some sign of tenderness—the tenderness that had been stirred in her by seeing him so vulnerable while she had been making love to him—but there was none.

'We've just become lovers and you don't even know who I am.' Something he was going to have to rectify—and as soon as possible, he realised, floundering. It was a feeling that was alien to Leonidas Vassalio.

'Yes, I do. Or as much as I need to,' she murmured, feeling his powerful body tense as she applied a trail of butterfly kisses over the slick warmth of his heavily contoured chest.

'I'm trying to be serious, Kayla.'

'Why?' she breathed against the velvety texture of his skin, delighting in the way his breathing was growing more and more ragged from her kisses.

But as her fingers trailed teasingly along the inside of one powerful thigh his hand suddenly clamped down on hers, resisting the temptation to let it wander.

'Because I don't believe you're the type of girl who does this without knowing what sort of man she's getting herself involved with and without demanding some degree of emotional commitment.'

And he wasn't offering any. She couldn't understand why telling herself that caused her spirits to plummet the way they did.

'I'm not demanding anything,' she uttered, knowing that the only way to save face was to get the hell out of there. 'And I'm sorry if I offended you!'

Scrambling out of bed, managing to shrug off the hand that tried to restrain her, she heard his urgent, 'Kayla! Kayla, come back here!'

She didn't, though. Her wounded pride propelled her into the adjoining bathroom, her mind focussed only on tidying herself up and getting out.

Stung with regret for upsetting her, momentarily Leonidas flopped back against the pillows. He hadn't intended her to take what he had said in the way she had. He had been trying to explain, in a roundabout way, what he should have told her long before, but procrastinating had only made an awkward situation far more difficult. After what had just happened he didn't know how or where to begin. He only knew that he couldn't let it happen again before he told her the truth—and all he'd managed to do was let her believe she'd offended him...

Offended him! He couldn't stop a lazy smile from touching his mouth.

She'd blown his mind, he thought, when she'd woken him up from a deep, deep sleep and dragged him straight into a cauldron of sizzling pleasure. He hadn't had time to catch his breath—let alone think! And he wouldn't have been caught so off-guard, still in bed, if he hadn't been up practically all night trying to get round one last hitch with those amended plans...

The plans!

He shot up in bed just as Kayla was emerging from the bathroom.

He'd left all his paperwork spread out over the kitchen table with his laptop—incriminating evidence of who he was! It had been late, and he'd obviously crashed out on the bed after he'd come up here and showered!

'Kayla, come here!'

The authority in his voice would have stopped a lesser mortal, but she ignored it as she moved around the bed, frowning, tugging at the draping folds of the bedlinen.

'Are you looking for something?' he asked, knowing he had to act quickly.

Kayla made a grab for the red briefs he was holding up, which only succeeded in bringing her across the bed and against his disturbingly masculine body as he withheld them, effectively securing what he wanted.

'You haven't offended me. You were wonderful,' he murmured, his warm breath a delicious sensuality against her hairline. 'Now, come back to bed. I want to talk to you,' he said, and just as an incentive slipped his hand under the tantalising little skirt and let his fingers play along the outer curve of one taut, silky buttock.

Kayla groaned, weakening beneath his mind-boggling powers of persuasion. She felt vulnerable and incredibly sexy with no panties on, but she despaired at herself too, at how easily and effortlessly he could bend her to his will.

Whatever he had to say, she had the strongest suspicion that she wasn't going to like it. He didn't want commitment. Of course he didn't. And anyway she wasn't ready for another serious relationship yet. Yet neither was she ready to let him have it all his own way.

Catching him in an unguarded moment, reaching round to adjust the pillows behind them, she managed to wriggle out of his arms and snatch her underwear from his grasp, saying, 'I can talk better over a cup of coffee,' as she ran giggling out of the room.

'Kayla, come here!'

She was in the hall, pulling her panties back on, when he raced down the stairs, still fastening his robe, but darted off again laughingly as soon as she saw him coming.

'Will you just stand still and let me talk to you?'

he called after her as she grabbed the carrier bag she'd left on the chest and headed for the kitchen. He had to break it to her gently. She'd be angry, it was true, but not as angry as she would be finding it out for herself.

'Go and sit down,' he commanded softly when she turned around. He was pointing to the sitting room. 'I will make the coffee.'

'Fine,' she agreed airily, pivoting away again, 'but I'll keep you company while you're doing it.'

'In the sitting room,' he breathed, in one last attempt to prevent her from seeing all his papers.

She turned in the kitchen doorway, her chin lifting in playful challenge. 'And since when did you suddenly start issuing so many orders?'

'Since I thought you were running out on me without finishing what you started.' One purposeful stride brought him over to her, his mouth a sensuous curve. But inside he was a heaving mass of turmoil.

He had to keep her out of the kitchen—stop her going in there before he had a chance to explain. He cast a surreptitious glance over her shoulder at the table in the centre of the room, heaving with incriminating evidence. He should have told her before. Should have kept her in bed...

'Kayla…'

The way he spoke her name never failed to turn Kayla's bones to jelly.

'Say it again,' she murmured huskily.

'What?' He looked tense, she thought, and mystified too.

'The way you say my name.'

'Kay-lah.'

She groaned her satisfaction and nestled against his chest above the gaping V of his dark satin robe. His skin smelled of the lingering traces of shower gel overlaid with a sensual musk.

'It should be censored—or at least X-rated,' she purred, with her tongue coming out in a provocative caress of that bared skin. It felt silky and tasted slightly salty…

Dear heaven!

Leonidas dragged in a breath, at a loss for the words he needed to say. He didn't know what powers this girl used to bewitch him, but even as he struggled to engage his normally incisive brain his body was responding with an urgent message of its own. It was taking all the mental strength he possessed not to rip down her panties, lay her down right here on the marble floor and enjoy the pleasure of having her beneath him, with himself in the driving seat this time. But he *had* to get her out of this room!

Swiftly his mouth swooped down over hers in a bid to distract her enough to manoeuvre her back into the hall. But he hadn't reckoned on how distracting her soft mouth would be to him.

Feeling her warm body against his, he could only respond to it in a kiss that went on and on, until they both came up for air and her head dropped back against his shoulder.

A few moments later, lifting her head, she murmured, 'What is that?'

Leonidas's spine pulled into a tight, tense rod. All he had succeeded in doing was turning her round, so that their positions were reversed, and she was now looking at the plans he'd set up on an easel. Allowing her to pull out of his arms, he felt the slaying blow of defeat.

Stepping down into the kitchen and dumping the bread bag on the table, bewildered, Kayla couldn't take it in. There were papers. Lots of papers. A laptop and a memo pad. And what she had thought were sketches looked like some sort of plan...

'What is it?' Her eyes skittered from the easel to the table and then the briefcase standing open on the floor. 'Is it something you're working on? Some building work…?'

Leonidas took a step towards her. 'Kayla, I can explain.'

'Explain?' She looked at him with confusion in her questioning blue eyes. 'Explain what?'

What was he doing with what looked like a whole set of plans for some development scheme? And a big, *big* development scheme by the look of it, she realised, when her gaze swept back over the table. Something proposed by the Vassalio Group—a big, *big* developer. She knew that much as her eyes took in the recognisable black and gold logo at the top of the plan she was staring at.

'I don't understand…' Why had his cosy farmhouse kitchen taken on the look of some executive's pad? Why was he looking so serious?

At that moment his cell phone rang from somewhere, shrilling across the sudden pregnant silence.

He pulled it out of the pocket of his robe, his eyes never leaving hers as he intoned incisively, 'Vassalio.' And then the penny dropped.

It was like an unashamed declaration directed specifically at her, Kayla thought, realising she had started to tremble.

Vassalio. Leon. Leonidas Vassalio. She knew the name. Of course she did! She'd heard it often enough in the media, seen the company logo on billboards and advertising for commercial developments, but she'd never taken much notice of it until now.

'You lied to me,' she accused in a virtual whisper when he cut the call short, feeling so shocked and betrayed that it was almost painful to breathe. 'You've lied to me ever since I got here!'

'Misled,' he corrected as he dropped his phone back into his pocket.

As if it made a difference!

'Most of it was what you assumed.'

'Hah! Like I assumed I knew who you were when we were doing what we were doing just now?'

Leonidas Vassalio. The man she had just taken advantage of—and who had let her!

'How could you do it?' She was referring to the sex, shame creeping over her, scorching her already flushed cheeks. What a laugh he must have been having—and at her expense!

'You didn't give me much choice,' he reminded her dryly.

'You could have stopped me any time you wanted to!'

'Really?' A sceptical eyebrow arched sharply.

'You think I'm that superhuman?' His mouth twisted in hard self-derision. 'Show me any red-blooded man you think would be capable of resisting being dragged out of sleep by a sex-goddess with no panties on.'

He made her feel cheap, and she wished fervently that she could turn back the clock instead of just standing there, hating herself for feeling the burn of desire stir deep down inside her where she was still moist and slightly tender from their spontaneous and unrestrained coming together.

'If it makes you feel any better,' he said, running fingers through his long dishevelled hair, 'I didn't intend for things to go as far as they did.'

'Oh, really?' she shot back, her features distorted with self-disgust. 'What a bonus it must have been for you when they did!'

'It wasn't like that.' He sounded defensive, exasperated—angry, almost. 'Why the hell do you think I didn't take things to their natural conclusion the other day on that island?'

'Because it was more fun stringing me along.'

'That isn't true.'

'Isn't it? And what about just now? You wouldn't have thought twice about doing it again.'

'That wasn't my motive,' he stated decisively. 'I

was trying to coax you into the sitting room so that I could break it to you gently who I am without it flaring up into the mess we find ourselves in now.'

'You mean instead of me finding out for myself what a rotten lying cheat you really are?'

'If that's what you want to believe,' he rasped, grim-mouthed. 'But it was never my intention to deceive you.'

'Why?' It was a small cry from somewhere deep down inside of her. 'Why should I believe anything you say?'

'All right. I deserve that,' he accepted with no loss of dignity. He clearly wasn't a man to grovel or to eat humble pie. 'Look, I apologise for not telling you before now,' he continued. 'But I didn't know who you were when you first arrived. For all I knew you were a snooping journalist on a mission for a story, and I came here for some privacy. To get away from all the media attention and publicity that's been dogging me over this past year. I wasn't going to risk losing all that for a girl I didn't even know. Apart from which, I found it rather refreshing being with someone who wasn't playing up to me because of the size of my bank balance.'

'So you used me!' Kayla breathed. 'Just for your own amusement.'

'That isn't what I'm saying. But if you want to think that, then there's nothing I can do to stop you.'

'You could have trusted me enough to tell me the truth!'

He made a self-deprecating sound down his nostrils. 'A man in my position can't afford to trust.'

'Which just goes to show the type of people you mix with,' she tossed back, refusing to give any quarter. He had lied to her. Deceived her. And, though it was killing her to acknowledge it, that made him no better than Craig.

'I can't argue with that,' Leonidas conceded. 'But I don't suppose it would make any difference to tell you that you don't fall into their category.'

'You mean because none of the others have been such a push-over as I've been?' Near to tears, it came out almost on a sob, but there was no way in a million years that she was going to let him see that. Forcing aggression into her voice, she uttered, 'A builder. Hah! You must have been laughing up your exclusive designer sleeve!'

Ignoring that last remark, he said, 'That was your interpretation when I said I was in construction— which, as you can see...' he gestured to the plans on the easel, the others on the table '...I *am*.'

'And you let me think it! That's worse than lying! That's…'

'Kayla, stop it!' He made a calming gesture with his hands. 'I can understand how you must feel.'

'Can you?' Her eyes were dark and tortured, and her mouth was twisted in wounded accusation. No wonder he'd got nasty about her taking photographs of him in the beginning!

'I've said I'm sorry, haven't I?'

'And you think that makes it all right? An apology from the great Leonidas Vassalio!' Her bitter little laugh made him visibly wince.

'No, it doesn't make it all right.' Beneath the robe his tanned chest fell in hopeless frustration. He hadn't intended it to sound as dismissive as it had come out. 'I was constantly aware that I was going to have to tell you sooner or later.'

'Oh, really?' Kayla shot him a look of pure incredulity. 'Like when, exactly? After we'd had sex again?'

'Kayla, stop it!' He was moving towards her, but she backed away.

'So how did you imagine I'd respond?' She'd come up against a chair, the one where she'd sat that morning after he'd rescued her from the villa, but she didn't want to think about that now. 'By being grateful to you?'

'Which is exactly why I've never said anything,' Leonidas admitted raggedly.

'Because it would have spoilt your fun!'

'Because I didn't want to hurt you.'

'Oh, you wouldn't have hurt me, Leon!' Hadn't she been hardened by Craig? And before that her father? she reflected bitterly, before tagging on with painful cynicism, 'I'm sorry. *Is* it Leon? Or should that be Leonidas now?'

The emphatic distaste she placed on the name everyone knew him by made him flinch. But he couldn't blame her, he thought. He had misled her, and then been stupid enough to imagine he might be let off lightly when he came clean and admitted it. But she had been hurt too deeply before and he should have known better, he realised. It was crass of him to have thought she would be anything but angry and bitter, especially after finding out in the way she had.

'You wouldn't have hurt me, Leonidas,' she reiterated, in an attempt to ease the pain of another betrayal—and by a man she had believed was different from men like Craig and her father and all the others. A construction worker who'd come here to fish and sketch and live rough for a while because he valued his solitude and his privacy. Except all the time she'd been naïve enough to imagine he'd been sketching he'd been controlling his multi-billion-pound empire! 'I just wouldn't have touched you with a bargepole.'

But she had, she thought bitterly, remembering just how eagerly she had touched him—with her mouth and her hands and her whole reckless and stupidly trusting body. Tears stung her eyes as she thanked her lucky stars that she hadn't quite suc-ceeded in giving him her heart as well.

'Kayla…' He made another move towards her, but she backed away again, knocking the chair into the table this time and pushing some of his papers askew. 'I'm still the same person I was when you were driving me wild for you upstairs.'

'No, you're not! You're as bad as every other *company man*—' she breathed it with venom '—I've ever met. Only worse. Because you've ar-rived! And to think I was trying to suggest things you could do to make life better for yourself!' She couldn't believe she could have been so stupid. Such an unbelievable fool!

'Which I found very endearing,' he added ear-nestly.

'Don't touch me!' She made a small panicked sound as he took another step towards her, the thought of what his lips and hands could do to her exciting her in a way that made her feel sick with herself. 'You know exactly what I think about men like you!'

'Then we've both been misguided,' he concluded, his shoulders drooping, suddenly seeming to give up trying to placate her. 'You for taking everything at face value, and I for imagining I could get away with letting you. I just wanted to believe that for a while at least my name and my money weren't the most important things about me.'

There was something in his voice that had her silently querying the inscrutable emotion in that strong, rugged face. 'Is that supposed to make me feel bad?' she challenged. 'Because it doesn't.'

'No. I've already told you,' he persisted. 'It wasn't my intention to hurt you, or to let things go as far as they did.'

'And what about Philomena?' Her gaze had fallen to the bag with the loaf the woman had lovingly baked for him. 'Does *she* know?' she threw at him, hurting, remembering how eagerly she had driven up here to see him, with nothing but making him want her on her mind. 'Does she know what a fool you've been taking me for? Or didn't you risk telling her?'

Thick black lashes came down over his incredibly dark eyes. 'I've never taken you for a fool,' he stated, exhaling deeply. 'As for Philomena...she knows I had my reasons.'

'And she went along with them?' She couldn't believe that of the gentle yet down-to-earth Philomena.

'What do you think?' he said.

She remembered the argument that had ensued the day he'd first taken her down to the cottage, the remonstrations by Philomena since, which seemed to leave him no more than mildly amused.

'You're despicable,' she breathed, as a fragment of memory tugged at her consciousness in relation to something he had said about having had a trying year.

Unscrupulous. Ruthless. Riding roughshod over people. Those were words she had heard in connection with the name Leonidas Vassalio. And then she remembered. It was that stunning American model turned actress—Esmeralda Leigh. She'd publicly named him as having fathered her child. It was she who had called him unscrupulous, when he had challenged the proof of his paternity—

though there had been no close-up photograph of him in the article Kayla remembered reading. Just a long shot of him leaving his office, looking rather different from how he looked now, which had been inset in a full-colour spread of Esmeralda lounging in the drawing room of her exquisitely and expensively furnished Mayfair home.

'Esmeralda was right. You *are* unscrupulous!'

'And if you had read the outcome of that fiasco you would have the sense to realise that anything the woman says is fabricated. Her claims were proven to be totally untrue.'

'Well, she wasn't the only one who was good at lying, was she?' Kayla reminded him grievously, realising now what he'd meant that day when he'd referred to a petition being slapped on him. 'Was it because of her that you decided to get your own back when you met me? Were you afraid if I knew who you were I might try and get pregnant so I could use you as a ticket to an easy life? Well, stuff your money! And stuff *you!* Not everyone puts as much value on money as on truth and integrity! I might not be in your league when it comes to material wealth, but at least I can hold my head up and know that what you see is what you get. That everything about me is real. You wouldn't understand that if it was scrawled all over one of your concrete eyesores, and as far as I'm concerned, Mr Vassalio, I never want to see you again!'

CHAPTER EIGHT

'I HAD HOPED your time in Greece would make you feel better,' remarked Yasmin Young, an abrupt and artificially blonde forty-five-year-old to Kayla, who had just come downstairs and declined her mother's offer to cook her breakfast. 'But ever since you've been back you haven't eaten properly. You're too thin. And you've been going around like someone who's lost a shilling and found sixpence. I was right when I said you were unwise, cutting your holiday short like that. I've told you before,' she reiterated, going over what seemed to Kayla like a mantra from her mother these days. 'He isn't worth wasting any more time over, you know. None of them are.'

She was talking about Craig. Kayla hadn't told her mother anything about meeting anyone while she had been away. But the maternal advice applied equally to how she was feeling about Leonidas—and had been ever since she'd returned to the UK on that wet and windy mid-May morning, hurting and feeling so gullible and betrayed. And all because she had been stupid enough to get herself emotionally involved with a man right out of the same mould as Craig, her father and all the others. Because she *had,* Kayla thought, berating herself—even if she had only realised it when it was too late.

'I know,' she responded now, even managing to feign a smile as she poured herself a hasty cup of coffee. She shook her head at her mother's concerned suggestion that she should at least try and eat some toast.

'I'd better go or I'll be late,' she said, rushing out of the door without bothering to finish her coffee.

At least she wasn't out of work and dependent upon her mother to help support her, she thought in an attempt to brighten herself up as she sat in heavy traffic on her way to work. At least she still had a job. And it promised to be a potentially permanent one if Josh and Lorna managed to land the huge contract they had been hoping to secure for the past few weeks.

It would be the break they needed and they were both beside themselves with excitement—particularly as their potential client was Havens Exclusive, a company that provided luxury homes and apartments for the higher end of the market. Kayla was keeping her fingers crossed for them both.

Without her having to worry about things like whether Kendon Interiors would still be trading this time next year, Lorna might have a chance with her pregnancy this time, she thought, hoping fervently that her friend would be able to carry this baby to full term. And being busy again could only be good for *her* too, Kayla decided, because apart from the satisfaction of being able to stay in a job she enjoyed, it helped keep her mind off Leonidas.

She hadn't heard from him since that morning she had stormed out of the farmhouse. Not that she'd wanted to, or even imagined that she would. He didn't know where to find her, for a start.

She'd wasted no time in leaving the island after driving back to Philomena's that last morning, having discovered that there was a ferry leaving that day.

'Leon…he good man,' Philomena, having guessed what had happened, had tried to tell her gently. He could act stupidly sometimes. Like most men! At least that was what the woman had seemed to be saying with her gestures and a world-weary rolling of her eyes.

Well, he hadn't shown any evidence of his virtuous qualities with *her!* Kayla seethed, still hurting from the way he had deceived her, even though it was more than six weeks on. She tried not to think about how he had rescued her that night in the storm and helped her with the clean-up operation the following day. Nor did she want to think about the affection he'd shown towards Philomena. Remembering just filled her with longing, and with such an aching regret that things couldn't have been different that at times it almost took her breath away. He was a rat when all was said and done. She didn't need him or want him! And she certainly never intended to be so taken in by anyone again! So why did she spend every waking moment trying not to think about him? Why did the thought of never seeing him again leave her feeling so down and depressed?

Fortunately the buzz around the office kept any further disturbing introspection at bay, since one of Havens' senior management team was coming in to meet with Josh and Lorna the following day.

'They've already been through our history and our previous trading figures, and now I think they just want to give us the once-over,' Lorna remarked anxiously. Her mid-length bobbed hair was coming out of the clips she had tried to fasten it with as she despaired of her devoted but untidy husband's muddle of an office. Like Kayla, she was blonde and petite—apart from her burgeoning middle—which was why they had often been taken for sisters, Kayla reflected fondly, knowing she couldn't have cared more for Lorna if she *had* been her sibling.

Consequently, having worked late to help tidy up Josh's office and prepare the conference room for what they hoped would be the final meeting, Kayla was getting ready to go home when the telephone rang in her office.

'Hello, Kayla.'

She almost froze, recognising Leonidas Vassalio's deeply accented voice at the other end of the line.

'How did you find me?' Stupid question. A man with his money and influence would have ways and means, she realised, her pulses leaping. Or had she told him where she worked? She couldn't even think clearly enough to remember.

'How have you been?'

She didn't answer but, aware that Josh and Lorna were still around somewhere in the building, moved over and closed the door. She'd been too hurt and ashamed of herself even to tell them that she had met someone in Greece, and she didn't want them finding out about it now.

'What do you want?'

'I'd like to see you.'

'Why?' she asked, breathless from the dark and sick responses suddenly surging through her.

'I would have thought that was obvious after the way you ran out on me that day,' he remarked dryly. 'So suddenly. Without a word.'

'What did you expect me to do?' she asked pithily, in spite of the way her heart was thudding. 'Stick around so you could make an even bigger fool of me?'

'It was never my intention to make a fool of you.' His voice had dropped a semi-tone to become almost caressing, reminding her of how treacherously it had excited her when she'd been deceived into believing he was someone else.

'No?' It came out sounding more wounded than she'd intended. 'I'd like to know what you'd have done if you'd really been trying.'

'Yes, well…'

His words tailed away on a heavily drawn breath while Kayla pictured him, wherever he was, his hair wild and untamed, looking as casual as he sounded in his automatic assumption that she would even consider seeing him again.

'I know you're still angry....'

'Whatever gave you that idea?' It came out on a shrill little laugh.

'Have dinner with me,' he suggested, amazing Kayla with his unerring confidence.

Even so, her heart leaped traitorously in response.

'Why?'

In the moment's silence that followed she imagined a masculine eyebrow tweaking at her challenging response.

With more composure than she was managing to retain, he answered, 'Because we have things to discuss.'

'Oh, really? Like what?' She could hear Lorna and Josh still working in the conference room above—moving chairs, closing windows for the night—as she pushed her loose hair behind an ear with a shaky hand. 'Like why you made a complete idiot out of me in Greece? Like why you pretended to be somebody you weren't when I was in trouble and needed help? And why you kept pretending even when I was taken in by you and offered you suggestions of what you could do with your life to improve your lot? Or is it the other thing you want to apologise for? For having sex with me when you were lying through your teeth and thinking I'd simply forgive you if I found out? Because *you're* the idiot if you think I'd go anywhere and discuss anything with you after what you did.'

'And that's all you have to say?' His voice was toneless now, devoid of any emotion.

'Why? Do you really want to hear some more?' She could feel the bite of tears behind her eyes but she willed them back. She couldn't cry. Couldn't let him hear how brutally he had hurt her and make an even bigger fool of herself into the bargain. 'Because there's a whole barrelful where that came from!' Resentment defended her from the pain he had inflicted upon her, the hurt to her pride, her trust and her emotions.

'I think I get the message,' he rasped under his breath. 'As the saying goes, see you around.'

He had rung off before she could even regain her wits.

Kayla was at the office early the following morning, to prepare the conference room for the important meeting. She had slept very little for thinking about Leonidas, but she hid her tiredness behind a bright façade as she put out pens and paper, tumblers and a jug of water, arranged fresh flowers for the centre of the long table and generally helped Lorna to stay calm.

Her friend was flitting around in a state of anxious excitement. Worried for her, Kayla insisted that she sat down and took a few deep breaths before the man from Havens arrived.

'Supposing after all this they don't think we're solid enough and change their mind about giving us their business?' Lorna said worriedly. 'Or they think we don't have enough expertise and decide to go with a company that's bigger and better?'

'Bigger, maybe—but not better,' Kayla assured her, meaning it. 'Anyway, you said yourself the contract's as good as in the bag. This meeting's only a formality, so stop worrying,' she advised gently. But secretly she *was* concerned.

Lorna was nearly six months pregnant now, and Kayla knew how much this coming baby meant to her and Josh. Lorna had to stay free from stress if this pregnancy wasn't to end in the same traumatic way as her previous two pregnancies had, and getting overwrought about anything was bad news.

Havens had said that they might require some extra financial information, and Kayla was pleased, therefore, that as their bookkeeper she had been asked to attend the meeting. It would help take the pressure off Lorna.

'You'll also serve as our charm offensive,' Josh had joked.

Consequently, when he rang down to her office at ten o'clock sharp and asked her to join them, Kayla slipped her charcoal-grey tailored suit jacket on over her sleeveless blue blouse and, checking the French pleat she'd carefully styled her hair in that morning, took the lift to the first floor, prepared to charm the Havens man for all she was worth.

'Come in, Kayla.' A quiet-voiced Josh—mousy beard neatly trimmed and looking unusually smart today in a jacket and tie—was standing at the top of the table. Lorna was sitting on his right. But it was the man who had been sitting opposite her and was now getting to his feet that made Kayla feel she'd suddenly been gripped by some hideous hallucination. Until Josh said, 'Kayla, this is Mr Vassalio. Mr Vassalio, this is our invaluable bookkeeper, Kayla Young.'

She wasn't sure how she managed to walk around the table to take the hand Leonidas was holding out to her. She felt stiff-backed and winded, and in the four-inch heels she hadn't given a second thought to wearing that morning, suddenly in danger of over-balancing.

'Miss Young.'

She didn't know what automatic response gave her the emotional strength to take his hand in the outward appearance of a formal handshake, or whether he could feel the way her fingers were trembling as he held them in his warm palm a fraction of a second too long.

'Mr Vassalio.' It came out as a croak from between lips that felt as dry as kindling, while flames seemed to be leaping through her blood—not just from the shock of his being there, but from his devastating appearance too.

Since she had last seen him he seemed to have changed his whole persona. The designer stubble was gone, as was the long, unruly hair. Now expertly cut, the jet-black layers waved thickly against a pristine white collar, although the mid-grey suit he wore, with its fine tailoring, could do nothing to tame the restless animal energy of the man beneath.

Clean-shaven, he looked harder—and even more dynamic, if that were possible. The evidence of the high-octane lifestyle he had disguised so well on the island was emblazoned on every hand-sewn stitch of his designer clothes. She had often thought him totally out of place in the run-down environs of the farmhouse. Today he was exactly where he belonged. Here, in the halls of business, he cut a figure of formidable power in his dress, his manner, and in the overwhelming authority he exuded.

Kayla couldn't think, paralysed by the dark penetration of his gaze and the mockery touching his stupendous mouth. When she did eventually manage to drag her gaze from his it was with a confused look at Josh, and she blurted out the first thing that came into her head.

'Not Mr Woods…?'

It was the wrong thing to say, and she realised it when she saw the dismayed look on Lorna's tense and nervous features. But it was with a Mr Woods that the appointment had been made.

'Woods couldn't make it.'

Leonidas's response drifted down to Kayla as though through a thick fog. She was hot and perspiring. Her clothes, so fresh and cool only minutes before, now seemed to be sticking to her.

'Mr Vassalio's the main man. Havens Exclusive is one of the companies within his group. He wanted to see us for himself,' Lorna told her. 'Isn't that right, Mr Vassalio?'

'Leonidas, please.' The smile he gave Lorna could have melted a polar ice-cap, and Kayla saw her friend visibly relax.

'Leonidas.' Smiling up into the perfect symmetry of his dark masculine features, Lorna repeated the name as if it was some sort of coveted trophy. She was positively glowing in the man's effortless charm, Kayla realised, wondering what her friend would say if she told her what a cheat he was. What a liar!

'Perhaps Miss Young would sit here...' he was already pulling out the chair beside his '...and fill me in on anything I might need to know.'

It was all purely a formality. Like his handshake, Kayla thought with a little shiver. She knew he would already have had Havens suss out their financial credibility and their ability to meet their commitments before he'd let one of his companies consider investing a penny.

But was this just a bizarre coincidence? Or had he specifically arranged for Havens to take advantage of Josh and Lorna's expertise, armed with the knowledge that she, Kayla, worked at Kendon Interiors? Had he known when he'd telephoned her last night that he'd be coming here today? If so, why hadn't he said so? Or had his intention been to give her the shock of her life? To get his own back for refusing to have dinner with him? Because if it had, he had succeeded. And how!

She couldn't stop her eyes from straying to him as he began talking business with Josh and Lorna. She couldn't help noticing how richly his hair gleamed in the light of the window behind him. Nor could she keep her ears from tuning in to the resonant tones of his voice, any more than she could stop the subtle spice of his aftershave lotion acting on her nostrils like some exotic aphrodisiac.

His hands were a magnet for her guarded yet brooding gaze—long, tapered hands that had made her cry out with their tender and manipulative skill. The dark silky hairs that peeped out from under an immaculate shirt cuff were an all too painful reminder of his dark and dangerous virility.

He had been stupendous before. Now he was no less than sensational! A man who would turn heads with his dynamism and that air of unspoken authority. A man who was wealthy and ruthless and powerful. She'd known that before she'd left the island. But this man she didn't know at all.

Seeing him in full corporate action, power-dressed and dominating everyone else in the room, she couldn't believe that this was the man she had taken the initiative with and pleasured so uninhibitedly that last morning, and it left her feeling as mortified as if she had tied him up first and chained him to the bed.

Except that this man could never be chained or dominated...

Heat suffusing her body, she looked up and met his eyes just as he was finishing saying something to Josh about the FT Index. From the smouldering burn of his gaze as it dropped to her fine blouse she knew he had guessed what she was remembering, and from the discreet curve of his mouth she knew, with shaming certainty, that he was remembering it too.

She was glad when the meeting was over, the terms of the contract finalised, and he was preparing to leave. Being polite and courteous for Josh and Lorna's sakes was beginning to tell on her nerves.

At least he would go now, she thought. And hopefully after today, after he gave Havens the go-ahead to start the process for the contract rolling, she would never have to see him again. She didn't know why that prospect failed to satisfy her as it should. In fact it left her surprisingly down-spirited.

She just wanted to get back to her office. Get stuck into spreadsheets and invoices and try to forget that Leonidas Vassalio had ever existed.

He was talking to Lorna about the baby, asking her when it was due. Seeing she was no longer needed, Kayla seized the opportunity to excuse herself, and was heading for the door when she heard deep Greek tones request, 'Could I presume upon you, Josh, to spare your Miss Young for a little while longer? There are one or two things I need to run through with her, if she'll be good enough to walk with me back to my car.'

Go to hell! Kayla wanted to toss back as she pivoted round. But of course she had to be on her best behaviour for her friends' sake. There was no way she was going to let them down.

'Take all the time you need,' she heard Josh saying amiably, unaware of the conflict going on inside her.

Leonidas was holding the door wide for her, his arm outstretched so that she had to duck underneath it, and her startling response to his raw and overpowering masculinity made her voice falter even as she sniped in a hostile whisper, 'Does everybody *always* jump over themselves to please you?' She was breathing shallowly, trying to shrug off her involuntary reaction to him, how the heady, tantalising scent of him affected her.

'Not everybody.' Amusement laced his tones, but there was something about the look he gave her which excited her even as she rebelled against the way it seemed to promise, *but you will.*

'Why didn't you tell me yesterday?' she remonstrated as soon as they were in the corridor of the modern office unit, keeping her attention on a large potted fern that was benefiting from the light from the wide windows.

'Tell you what?'

As if he didn't know!

'That you were coming here today.' She was acutely aware of him walking beside her.

'You didn't give me the chance.'

'Really?' Her head swivelled round from the view across the landscaped business park. 'I don't seem to recall you trying to bring it into the conversation.'

'For what other reason were you imagining I wanted to take you to dinner?'

Colour burned her cheeks at the hard edge to his voice. He was an executive now, Kendon Interiors' biggest client—or would be when that contract was signed—and with that remark he was reminding her of it in no uncertain terms.

'Then you should have made your motives more obvious.'

'Like you're doing now, in bringing me along here instead of using the lift?'

'I always prefer to use the stairs.'

'As you did on your way up?'

Of course, Kayla thought, realising that she had walked right into that one. She should have known that his keen brain would have been attuned to every sound that had heralded her approach. He would have heard the ping of the lift and the door gliding open only seconds before she had come into the room.

'What's wrong, Miss Young?' His deliberate use of her surname seemed mockingly incongruous with the electricity that was crackling between them. Even the light click of her heels against the comparatively sturdy tap of his over the polished floor seemed to stress the glaring differences in their sexualities. 'Don't you want to chance the two of us being alone together in a lift?'

Kayla's heart seemed to stop when he opened the

glass fire door onto the next level and her jacket brushed his sleeve as he let her through.

'Why are you flattering yourself that I'd let that bother me?'

'Because if you could read my mind, Miss Young, you'd know that I have the strongest urge right now to rip that prim little suit off your body, followed by your blouse and then your—'

'Do you mind?' Her heels clicked more agitatedly at all he was suggesting as they came down onto the ground floor. From behind her desk the young receptionist smiled at them as they passed, her eyes feasting appreciatively on Leonidas.

'Modesty, Miss Young?' Though his mouth was twitching at the corners, he kept his eyes on the external glass doors, which slid open to admit them into the morning sunshine. 'I hadn't noticed any of that when you were bouncing up and down on my bed.'

'Stop it!'

'Why? Can you dismiss it that easily?' he tossed at her, sounding more impatient now. 'Because I can't. Or are you saying you've forgotten just how much pleasure we gave each other?'

'I thought there was something you particularly wanted to discuss with me?' she parried huskily as her memory banks seemed to burst with erotic images of their time together before she'd found out who he was, that he had lied. 'If there isn't, then I'll get back to my office. I do have things to do, you know.'

'So do I.' His words came out on a harsh whisper.

They had reached his car: a sleek dark monster of a thing that put every other vehicle in the car park into the shade. This statement of his wealth and importance was something Kayla should have expected. Nevertheless, it still managed to knock her metaphorically sideways.

Stupidly, when he had phoned her last night, she had half envisaged him calling from his truck. But the truck belonged to Leon. Leon the drifter, who chopped logs and caught his own lunch and made sketches of her on a whim like some care-free, exciting bohemian. Or pretended to, she remembered, hurting. But this piece of expensive machinery belonged to Leonidas, Chief Executive of the Vassalio Group. International tycoon. The grandest player in the company man's arena.

'You look pale,' he commented in a surprisingly soft voice, his eyes tugging over features she knew looked sallow beneath her tan, taking in the dark smudges under her eyes. 'And thinner. Have you been overworking?'

'Not particularly,' she answered, and felt his dark scrutiny reawakening every aching hormone in her body. *I've just been lying awake at night, wondering how I'm ever going to forget you!*

His gaze had dropped to her middle and a cleft appeared between his eyes. 'You aren't…?' His meaning was obvious.

'Pregnant?' Kayla quipped curtly.

A furore of emotions seemed to cross his strong features and for one crazy moment she wished she could tell him that she was. Not because she wanted his baby. Or did she? The thought came like a bolt out of the blue. Surely she couldn't…?

She pushed the notion aside, refusing even to go there.

No. She would have just liked to see him rocked off his axis. Taken down a few degrees from his arrogant assumption that he could come here and—what? Take up from where they had left off? But she couldn't lie, couldn't deceive or hurt anyone the way he had deceived and hurt her.

'No, I'm not. Foolish though you might have thought me, I wasn't *that* foolish. Or mercenary,' she tagged on after a moment, thinking of the adverse publicity he had been subjected to by the famous Esmeralda. And to what end? To try and hang on to a man she couldn't bear to let go?

Was that relief in those spectacular eyes of his? She couldn't be sure. Nor could she understand why she felt such a bone-deep emptiness inside as she watched him open the passenger door of the car with one inconsequential movement of the remote control mechanism.

'Get in,' he commanded softly.

'No.' She was trembling from his nearness and everything his determination implied. But he was standing between her and the door he had just opened, and with the car in the next bay effectively blocking her route she couldn't escape without causing a scene.

'I said get in,' he rasped. 'Or, so help me, I'll start ripping off those clothes of yours here and now and make love to you in front of this whole blasted building! So what is it to be, Miss Young?'

She wanted to call his bluff. To resist getting into his car and falling victim to her own weakness for him, which would leave her hating herself for letting him use her as Craig had used her, for continuing to let him take her for a fool. She had a worrying suspicion, though, that if she did he would be quite capable of carrying out his threat. And so, reluctantly, with her heart beating wildly, she complied.

CHAPTER NINE

As Leonidas got in and started the car Kayla's nerves were stretched to breaking point.

Where was he taking her? As he put the car in motion she was so dangerously drawn to his dark magnetic presence that she didn't know how she would respond if he intended to do all he had threatened.

There were trees and bushes throughout the business park, separating units identical to the one that Kendon Interiors occupied. Kayla shot an anxiously challenging look at Leonidas as he brought the car around the trees to the last unit, which was still unoccupied, and cut the engine, leaving her tense and rigid at their screaming privacy.

'Tell me this is just some bizarre coincidence,' she implored him, her voice shaking. 'Your coming here today.'

'If you're asking if your friends approached my company with their business, then I'd like to say yes. But as it was my not being entirely honest with you that created a situation where I've had to virtually kidnap you to get you to talk to me, then I have to tell you that we brought our business to them. When you unintentionally made me aware of what Kendon Interiors were about it interested me, and I wanted to find out more. The company whose custom they lost because of the economic downturn are an old established company and well-known to me, and I knew they wouldn't have been dealing with your friends' business if what they had to offer wasn't a cut above the average in their field. Havens needed a new design company, and having had Kendon Interiors vetted over the past few weeks I liked what I saw and recommended them to my directors at Havens.'

'And you knew I'd still be working for them, of course?'

'With what amounted to a virtual rescue package in the shape of a potential and very valuable client on the table, your redundancy seemed pretty unlikely,' he drawled.

So he *had* been listening to her that day on that beach when he'd seemed preoccupied with what he had been scribbling in his notebook—and had acted on it! Nothing would escape this man.

'So you used what I told you about Josh and

Lorna's difficulties and deliberately set out to get them on your books just so you could get to me? That's stalking!' she accused heatedly.

'I prefer to call it a good corporate move,' he corrected. 'And while you drove me nearly insane in the bedroom, Kayla, I think you should be aware right here and now that I never let passion of any kind rule my head. Do you really think I'd let a company of mine waste money on a product they didn't need? A product that wasn't going to be of enormous benefit to me financially? I'm a businessman, Kayla, first and foremost. And while I can't deny that advising Havens to use Kendon Interiors' skill and expertise does generate some secondary benefits, my corporate interests are what concern me over and above anything else.'

'If by "secondary benefits" you mean getting me back into bed, forget it!' Kayla retorted, with her pulses racing.

'I was referring to the benefits to Kendon Interiors,' he returned phlegmatically.

Why did she have to open her mouth and put her foot in it again?

Abashed, Kayla sank back against the cushioning black leather with her eyes pressed closed, her hair a pale contrast against the headrest.

'You never cease trying to make me feel uncomfortable, do you?' she expressed in a censuring whisper.

'Quite unintentionally, believe me,' he answered, almost as softly. 'I think it's this unnatural denial by you of everything there is between us that is responsible for it.'

'There's *nothing* between us,' she refuted, knowing that in doing so she was guilty of doing exactly what he was accusing her of. Everything that was feminine in her was craving those strong arms around her again.

'No?' he queried, with such a wealth of meaning that her eyes flew open in guarded challenge.

He was looking at her without restraint, his eyes glittering with dark desire as they touched on the fullness of her trembling mouth. She felt her breathing grow shallow, felt an excruciating need at the very core of her as his heated gaze slid down to the silvery blue of her blouse, and her breasts rose and fell sharply in traitorous betrayal of her emotions.

'Leonidas...'

It was the first time she had spoken his full name without penetrating sarcasm. It was a breakthrough, he thought, even if she did sound like an accused prisoner who had just realised that any further denial of her crime was useless. Or perhaps she couldn't fight this thing that was making her so tense and cagey, that was driving him almost insane with the need to have her.

Scarcely daring to trust himself, he trailed a finger lightly along the silky texture of her jaw and heard her breath shudder brokenly through her lungs.

'Is that a plea?' he enquired huskily, feeling the ache in his body intensify in throbbing response.

No, it isn't! Kayla wanted to cry out in protest—except that the feelings he was arousing were preventing her from saying a thing.

'What do you want?' she asked falteringly at length, not daring to look at him. If she did then she'd be lost, she realised, despairing at herself. And she couldn't lose herself to him again—not after the last time. Not after the way he had treated her.

'I want us to finish what we started,' he said, amazing her with his arrogance and yet making her go weak in spite of everything. But at least he wasn't touching her any more.

'Why? Did you fall madly in love with me in

Greece and realise you can't live without me?' she suggested with bitter poignancy.

There was a far too lengthy pause before he answered.

'Only fools and adolescents fall madly in love,' he responded dismissively, and his cynicism was stinging even though it was no less than she would have expected from him. 'But I have to admit to having acted entirely out of character with you. You think you know me, but you don't, and I intend to show you exactly who Leonidas Vassalio is.'

'And how do you propose to do that?'

'By asking you to stay with me under my roof for a few weeks. In fact I'm insisting upon it.'

'Insisting?' He sounded so sure of himself, as though he wouldn't take no for an answer, that Kayla viewed him with a guarded question in her eyes. 'You're joking, surely?'

'On the contrary,' he said. 'I've never been more serious in my life. I think it would be a good idea if you move in tomorrow.'

'And if I don't?' It was a breathless little challenge, and one that he didn't take up immediately.

He didn't know why it was so imperative to keep this girl in his life—only that he had to. And if bending her to his will was the only way to do it, then so be it, he determined grimly.

'It would be a pity,' he expressed now. 'Especially as Josh and Lorna imagined we were all getting on so well. But starting a partnership of any kind without total harmony all round doesn't augur very well for future business.'

What was he saying? She wasn't sure, but she had a very good idea.

Though he wasn't actually telling her to her face, she felt sure that he would use Josh and Lorna's difficulties as a lever. The contract wasn't signed yet, and he could use his influence on Havens to get them to withdraw from supplying Kendon Interiors with their greatly anticipated custom. And if that happened...

Mortified, she breathed, 'You'd rescind that contract and see a business go down the drain if I don't do exactly what you're asking?' For what other reason would he have so miraculously sought Josh and Lorna out—regardless of what he'd said—if it wasn't to use their company's problems to his advantage?

His eyes, as she finished speaking, were darkly reflective, giving nothing away.

'Well, since you seem to know me so well...'

He didn't finish. He didn't have to, Kayla thought bitterly, staring with hurt, disbelieving eyes across a patch of manicured lawn to the vacant unit in front of which they were parked. A 'TO LET' sign was pinned to its rendered fascia. The place looked dark. Empty. Soulless.

Like he was, she thought achingly, and knew she had fallen in love with him back there on that island. In love with a man she hadn't even known...

A bell rang in her mind, reminding her of something he had said that last day after they had made love, but she pushed the memory aside. She didn't need anything that threatened to topple the barrier she had been forced to erect against him. Yet when he caught her chin between his thumb and forefinger and turned her head to look at him just the touch of that broad thumb sliding sensuously across her mouth almost broke her trembling resolve.

'Open your eyes,' he commanded softly.

When she did she saw something in his face that for a moment seemed to mirror her anguish—some emotion that burned with a dark and almost painful intensity. But then it was gone, like the extinguishing of a light, and his features seemed only to harden as he leaned forward, tilting her chin higher until there was just a hair's breadth between his mouth and hers.

His scent and his nearness were killing her. She wanted...

Oh, dear heaven! She wanted him! Even knowing what he was like. Even after the way he had deceived her! All she could think about was being naked in his arms and making love with him until...

She pressed her eyes closed to try and blot him out. A traitorous sensual tension gripped her. His breath was warm against her mouth, and the heady spice of his shaven jaw was acting like a powerful drug, stripping her of her will and her power to resist, until without even being aware of it she was leaning into him, her lips parting involuntarily to receive his kiss.

'No.' In an instant he was pulling back. 'Now isn't the time—and this certainly isn't the place.' His breathing came raggedly through his lungs. 'There will be ample opportunity in the future, I promise you. But in the meantime, if you're going to get to know me, *hrisi mou,* somehow I don't think we're going to achieve it like this.'

The sensual snub left her bruised and angry with herself—for feeling such bitter disappointment as

well as for allowing him to see how much she still
wanted him physically. It just showed him, once
again, how he had the power to humiliate her just
by turning her into a yearning, quivering wreck.

'I don't need to get to know you, Leonidas Vassalio. I know exactly what you are. You're playing games with me for your own amusement! And
you're using my friends to exploit the situation, no
matter how you might try to dress it up! All right.
I'll go along with your little game.'

If she didn't, and Havens withdrew their offer,
Kendon Interiors would be plunged straight back
into the difficulties they'd been facing before. And
if that happened, if Lorna was subjected to more
stress during her pregnancy… Kayla shivered, unable to bear thinking that the safety of a baby's little life might easily be in her own hands.

'I'll move in with you,' she conceded, in a voice
clogged with emotion, 'but I'm not sleeping with
you, if that's what you're imagining. I'm only doing
it for Josh and Lorna's sake, so don't you ever forget that—and don't imagine for one moment that
I'm going to enjoy it.'

'I wouldn't be so presumptuous,' he assured her
with mockery in his eyes. 'And now I'm going to

take you back. Your firm has a proposed contract to fulfil...'

The sudden seriousness of his tone served to remind her of exactly what he was—a typical high-flying executive, ruthless and manipulative, like all the rest she'd known.

'And they're not going to fulfil it if one of their principal staff is out testing her luck by antagonising their biggest client.'

Of course. He had the upper hand and he knew it, Kayla thought, shooting back nevertheless, 'Is that a threat?'

'Why not go the whole hog and call it blackmail?' he suggested smoothly. 'I'm sure you'd prefer to.' When she didn't answer, 'Tomorrow,' he reminded her, as he brought his powerful car around to the front entrance of Kendon Interiors. 'I'll pick you up at eight.'

The pool threw back reflections of the dazzling white mansion. A modern house, built to Georgian design, Leonidas's principal UK home was a breathtaking showcase of large airy rooms, all exquisitely furnished, combining modern with Regency and luxury with unfaltering good taste. A rich man's castle, presided over by a resident staff who catered for this king of enterprise with un-stinting respect and affability, as if he was more to them than just the man who paid their wages.

Now, lying beside the luxurious pool in equally luxurious grounds before it was time to get ready for the company dinner to which he was taking her tonight, Kayla was forced to accept, from what she'd observed over her first couple of days in his spectacular house, that the respect shown between Leonidas Vassalio and his staff was entirely mutual.

'Are you ready?' he asked two hours later, as she emerged from the suite of rooms he had assigned to her. It comprised a bedroom with floor-to-ceiling wardrobes, a four-poster bed and a carpet thick enough to drown in, a separate dressing room and a bathroom with a huge sunken tub within a setting of honeyed marble.

'I don't know,' Kayla responded, trying hard not to reveal how just the sight of him standing there at the top of the stairs in a dark evening suit and exquisitely fine shirt was making her blood sing with need. 'I'm your puppet. You tell me.'

He moved towards her like a dark panther, his equally dark eyes taking in every detail of her appearance.

She was wearing a strapless dress with a pale blue bodice that ran into a darker blue, the colour continuing down into purple and then burgundy as it swirled around her ankles. Silver high-heeled sandals gave him a glimpse of burgundy-tipped toes.

She'd twisted her hair up into a knot, leaving a few tendrils to fall softly around her face. Her only concession to cosmetics was a smudge of smoky-blue shading on her eyelids and a burgundy gloss enhancing her lips. Her long lustrous lashes, he was pleased to notice, she'd left naturally gold. Delicate spirals of silver hung from the lobes of her ears, matching the delicately twisted necklace that lay against her softly-tanned skin.

'You look beautiful.' For a moment it was all Leonidas could say. 'And you're not my puppet,' he countered when he had found his voice again. 'You're an independent-minded if not stubborn young woman whom I'm delighted to be accompanying tonight. If I'd wanted a puppet I wouldn't have had to travel too far to find myself a dozen of those.'

No, because every woman he knew would probably leap at the chance to do his bidding, Kayla thought. Whereas *she* was a woman who had walked away from him—said no to him when it had mattered—and that surely had to prove too much of a challenge for a man like Leonidas.

'Then you should have found yourself a dozen, shouldn't you?' she said, smiling brightly for the benefit of a manservant who was passing as they started down the magnificent staircase.

'Perhaps I should have,' he agreed, sounding mildly amused.

From the magnificent staircase to his magnificent car, to dinner in the ballroom of an equally magnificent hotel, Kayla was entranced but at the same time overwhelmed by the world he moved in. It was poles apart from that of the man he had purported to be—a man who had 'opted out', driven a wreck of a truck and bedded down in the run-down environs of a Greek farmhouse.

Here she saw a man at the very pinnacle of his prosperity. A man who lived and travelled in style and circulated with some of the most influential names in society. A man eloquent enough to hold an audience of over three hundred captive as he delivered an after-dinner talk on human complacency towards the state of the planet, leaving his peers congratulating him after a standing ovation that left him remarkably unfazed.

'You were brilliant,' Kayla remarked, unable to resist saying it as the tables were being cleared and couples were beginning to wander onto the dance floor to enjoy the middle-of-the-road music provided by a professional live band. She hadn't had a chance to speak to him since before he'd given the talk, and he'd been surrounded by many guests wanting to speak to him ever since.

'I was just stating fact and emphasising the responsibility that we as professional bodies should engage for the sake of our children and our children's children. We're only custodians of this earth. We don't own it,' he said. 'But am I to assume that I've hit on one topic that you're not going to flay me over tonight?'

With a change of tone he had wiped away her attempt to strike an equal balance with him if only for a few hours. Retaliation was futile, she decided. And anyway a smiling brunette, very glamorous and sophisticated, came up to him at that moment to thank him effusively, ogling him with such a blatant come-on in her sultry green eyes that there was no room for doubt as to exactly what she wanted from him.

'He's so eloquent!' she enthused to Kayla, daring to touch red-tipped fingers to his dark sleeve.

'He made my flesh go all goosebumpy just listening to him!'

'Really?' Kayla responded, trying to look impressed. 'Well, if that makes you goosebumpy then you should take a look at his sketches!' She felt the bunch of muscle in his powerful arm as she slipped hers through it in a gesture of pure possession. 'Of course he's very modest about them, but I'm sure he'd show them to you if you asked him nicely.'

Smiling uncertainly, the woman uttered something that Kayla didn't catch and, realising she was intruding, moved hastily away.

'I know you've got your grievances,' Leonidas rasped, as soon as his admirer was out of earshot, 'but do you have to air them in public? And what was *that* display of play-acting all about?' he queried, locking her arm against the sensuous fabric of his jacket as she would have pulled it away.

'I thought I was supposed to act as though I was enjoying being with you?' she murmured, with a bright smile for anyone who might be watching them.

He made a disapproving sound down his nostrils. 'You're behaving like every woman I went to Greece to get away from.'

Which was why he had been so careful not to

tell you who he was, her inner little voice piped up to remind her. But she didn't want reminding, and silenced the voice with the flash of another smile and a clipped, 'How do you *want* me to behave?'

'As Kayla Young. Guileless. Easy to like. And infernally inquisitive.'

'A fool,' she tagged on, all falseness gone. She was only aware then that he was leading her onto the dance floor. 'Guileless. Easy to like. And an infernally inquisitive, easy-to-fool fool!'

'How can I forget it?' he murmured, slipping those strong arms around her. 'You aren't prepared to let me.'

'Any more than I'm prepared to let you forget that I'm here under protest.'

'No, you aren't,' he purred silkily, drawing her close, sending Kayla's senses reeling in shaming response. 'I don't think "protest" can in any way account for the way we're both feeling now.'

This close to him she could feel every steel-hard muscle of his body—in the whipcord strength of his back and shoulders, in his hard hips and powerful thighs, and in the stirring evidence of his arousal. It made her want to press herself against him, and it took every shred of will-power she possessed not to do it.

'You aren't feeling anything. Just a bruised ego and severely dented pride because you can't bear a woman ever saying no to you.'

He laughed very softly, and with his cheek against hers whispered in her ear, 'Not a woman whom I know wants me as much as I want her— no.'

Even his breath was a turn-on against her treacherously pulsing flesh, without the stimulus of his stunning appearance and the way he'd had everyone there tonight eating out of his hand. It made her wish that they didn't have the baggage of the past hanging over them and that she was somewhere else, alone with him, not moving like this under an exquisite chandelier, with three hundred other people in the room.

'In fact, do you want to know what I think you are thinking now?'

The lights spun gold from Kayla's hair as she lifted her head in challenge. 'No,' she dismissed with a saccharine-sweet smile. 'But no doubt you're going to tell me anyway.'

'Well, let's see if I'm right,' he suggested. He was looking down at her and emulating her smile in a way that to anyone watching would have marked them undoubtedly as lovers—hungry for each other, wanting only the privacy of their bedroom. 'I think that right now you would prefer to be back at the house and for me to be slowly undressing you with some soft music playing. And I think you'd like me to remain clothed while I carry you naked up to my bed. There's nothing like the sensuality of cloth to add zest to lovemaking, is there, Kayla? Particularly when the man wearing it doesn't give a fig for how you might abuse it, just so long as he can gratify your desires and make you sob with pleasure.'

It was so close to what she had been thinking that Kayla could scarcely breathe. She could feel her cheeks burning from the shaming imagery. 'You're just indulging in your own uninhibited fantasies.' she croaked, her throat as arid as a Grecian hillside, and she felt those dark masculine eyes appraising the results of what his mind-blowing words had produced.

'Am I?' he challenged softly, with a knowing smile.

She wasn't even aware that the music had stopped until his arms fell away from her, and then she could see one of the older male guests to whom she'd been introduced earlier beckoning him from the bar.

'I'll be a few minutes,' Leonidas apologised, and left her to flee to the mercifully deserted sanctuary of the powder room.

A flushed-faced, bright-eyed creature stared back at her from the mirror above the luxuriously equipped basins. She felt as though she had just been aroused to fever-pitch only to be left abandoned and wanting. Wanting *him,* she acknowledged painfully, wondering how she still could.

How could she stay under his roof when every time he touched her it was like dropping a firework into a powder keg? When her common sense went up in smoke just at a look from him, even without the X-rated things he'd been saying to her just now?

And yet he hadn't attempted to touch her intimately since he'd brought her to his house—had merely treated her with a detached respect that had kept her awake over the past two nights wondering why he hadn't. Had he finally accepted that he had treated her unfairly and was now doing his best to make it up to her? Or was his plan to wear her down with the sort of earth-shattering sensuality he'd used just now until she was begging for him to make love to her?

She hadn't met a company man yet whose motives weren't entirely self-centred, so why should Leonidas Vassalio be any different? She rebuked herself for her moment of weakness in even daring to hope that he might be. Wasn't he using the plight of two people she cared about purely to satisfy his own selfish demands? And he'd already lived up to the type of man he really was in the way he had lied to her in Greece.

Even so, it was with a sick and building excitement that a little later she sat in the shadowy intimacy of his car, acutely aware of him sitting there beside her, changing gear with an immaculately cuffed wrist as he took a bend, driving them home, his jacket discarded in the back...

Only the hall light was burning on a dimmer switch as they came through the electronically operated gates and he admitted them into his magnificent house. Having watched the way he'd used his security card to open the impressively carved door, Kayla couldn't help comparing this man, with his millions and his discreet surveillance staff and his stringently guarded home, with the one who had slept with his doors unlocked—open to the world—alone on a lonely Greek hillside.

'Thanks. I think I'll go straight up,' she murmured, breathless with anticipation. She wasn't sure how she was managing to drag herself away from him as she started towards the wide sweeping stairs.

'Kayla...'

His soft command stopped her in her tracks, her heart beating a frenzied tattoo. If he touched her...

Dear heaven! She *wanted* him to touch her! To take the decision away from her, carry her up these stairs and drive her wild in the sumptuous luxury of his bed!

She turned round, her legs threatening to buckle under her. 'What?'

'You dropped your wrap,' he said, in a voice that was screamingly intimate.

Even the purposefulness of his tread on the pale marble was a sensuality that made her tense and yearning body throb.

Very softly he moved over and placed the blue and silver sequinned stole which she hadn't even realised had slipped off lightly over her bare shoulders. Then, with heart-stopping gentleness, he turned her round to face him.

He had retrieved his jacket since stepping out of the car, and the dark cloth now spanning his shoulders was a sensuality she wanted to touch.

It was a replay of all he had tormented her with

earlier, and she caught her breath, held in thrall by the scent and warmth and power of him as he stooped and pressed his lips against her forehead.

'You look tired,' he remarked, gazing down with some dark, unfathomable emotion at the naked hunger in her eyes. 'Get some rest,' he advised softly, leaving her excruciatingly lost and aching for him. 'We've got another busy day tomorrow.'

CHAPTER TEN

'WHY DIDN'T YOU tell me you were seeing him?' Lorna gasped, amazed, after Leonidas had telephoned Kayla in the office on Monday morning. 'And don't tell me you aren't, because that phone call certainly wasn't about trading figures! You're going out with him, aren't you?'

Imperceptibly, Kayla tensed. She hadn't told anyone that she was staying with Leonidas. All she had told her mother was that she was spending a couple of weeks with Lorna, and as Leonidas lived within a reasonable driving distance of Kendon Interiors, which meant that she could still come into the office, she had decided not to involve her friend in the lie.

'Don't spread it about,' she implored, reluctant to reveal her secret or to face the awkward questions that people would ask if she did.

What could she tell them, anyway? That she was only with Leonidas because he had made it impossible for her to refuse? That he was as good as blackmailing her to get her to comply with his wishes, and that she didn't intend staying in his house a second longer than after that contract was signed?

'If the paparazzi get wind of it they could turn his life into a circus,' she tagged on as casually as she was able to, although she was aware, from things Leonidas had already mentioned in passing, that they really could do just that.

'I won't. Well, only to Josh, of course,' Lorna stated unnecessarily. 'But how did you manage it? No, scrub that,' she put in hastily. 'You're smart and you're beautiful—he wouldn't have been worth his salt if he hadn't noticed you the moment you walked into the conference room last week. Wow! Won't that be one in the eye for Craig!' she continued, clearly flabbergasted. 'Honestly, Kayla! Do you *know* how rich he is?'

Rich and manipulative and using his power to get exactly what he wants, Kayla thought desolately. Because what he wanted was her, back in his bed. She was certain of that, despite the fact that he was making no advances to her in that respect, and regardless of how much he had hurt her—was still hurting her with his calculated plan to use her friends' precarious position as a lever to get her to fall in with him.

It was for that reason that she still couldn't bring herself to tell Lorna about meeting him in Greece. Lorna, who always thought the best of people, would instantly imagine that he had cast his company's business their way because Kayla had recommended them. She might even think he was doing it as a favour to her, Kayla, and she couldn't bear her friend to be deceived by him as she had, when nothing could be further from the truth.

'His money doesn't interest me,' Kayla tried to say nonchalantly, which produced a knowing little laugh from her friend.

'Well, no. I can see that there's far more that would interest you before you even got to his wallet! Gosh! If I wasn't married—and pregnant...'

'Which you are,' Kayla emphasised, managing a smile, knowing that her friend was only jesting. Lorna adored Josh, and her one desire in life was to give birth to their healthy baby. Dropping an almost envying glance to her dearest friend's burgeoning middle, Kayla decided right there and then that whatever it took to help Lorna fulfil that desire she would do, regardless of the cost to her own emotions.

* * *

During that week Leonidas went away on some unexpected business, returning a couple of days later to steal Kayla away early from the office and take her to a charity auction, where canapés were handed round on silver dishes and champagne flowed like water from a spring.

It was an event where the proceeds from the various items on offer went to a tsunami relief fund, and it soon became clear to Kayla that it was because of Leonidas's attendance and his company's support of the event that so many people had got involved.

'Did you enjoy that?' he asked her afterwards, when they were in the car, pulling away. 'As far as you were able to, of course, bearing in mind that your enjoyment level was probably stuck on zero in view of who you were with.'

Like her, he had refused the champagne after the first half-glass, and she was beginning to discover that his driving standards—as with most of what he did—were impeccable.

'Very amusing,' she remarked dryly, turning to look out of the window, secretly admiring the gardens surrounding the grand English country manor his company had hired to host the event. 'What was the object of the exercise in bringing me here today? To show me how charitable you can be?' She'd been surprised when he had paid over the odds for a small and not particularly well done watercolour of one of the local landmarks. 'There are those who might say you can afford to be.'

'You would be one of them, I take it?' When she didn't answer, already wishing she hadn't been so quick to snipe at him like that, he went on, 'It isn't about affording it, Kayla. It's about having enough clout to make others aware of the importance of events like this and bringing everyone together to contribute.'

Which he had done—and very successfully, she accepted, secretly impressed. Although she couldn't bring herself to admit it aloud, privately she couldn't deny that she had enjoyed herself—very much.

He took her to a West End show one evening—one she had wanted to see and for which she had been unable to get tickets. Afterwards, coming out of the exclusive restaurant where he had taken her for a late dinner, they were leapt on by photographers who almost succeeded in trampling her to death before Leonidas got her into the waiting limousine he'd had one of his aides bring to whisk them away.

'How do you cope with all this?' Kayla challenged, and he could tell from the all-encompassing gesture of her small chin that she meant the security and the car and the public demands his billionaire status made upon him, and not just the frightening intrusion of the paparazzi.

'One learns to live with it,' he said in a matter-of-fact voice, and then, more solicitously, asked, 'Are you all right?'

She nodded, but he could see that she wasn't. That anxious line between her eyes assured him that she was anything but happy being there with him. Also, being jostled by those photographers had caused the fine white silk of her dress to tear, and her beautiful hair, which she had styled so elegantly before they had left the house, was coming out of its combs. She looked as if she had been out in a gale—or with a far too impassioned lover.

The thought made him hard, but he steeled himself against it. She wasn't ready to accept him back into her bed just yet.

Consequently, when they reached the house he left her to go to bed alone and went straight to his study, where he spent hours catching up on some pressing paperwork in an endeavour not to give in to the almost overwhelming urge to mount the stairs two at time, rip back her bedcovers and watch her hollow protests dissolve beneath the surging demands of their entwined bodies.

The photographs were emblazoned across the tabloids the next day, with Kayla caught looking surprised and dishevelled and Leonidas urging her determinedly into the car.

'Have you seen them?' she wailed, ringing him on his mobile, having already spent half an hour on the phone, dodging awkward questions from her mother. She wasn't sure where he was, but her call had been diverted to his secretary first, who had obviously been asked to field his calls.

'Yes, I did, and I'm sorry,' he expressed, sounding annoyed over the publicity.

She was beginning to appreciate why he'd gone off to that island to escape it all for a while. Why he had been so angry when he had caught her supposedly taking photographs of him that first day.

'Say nothing,' he recommended, when she told him that someone from the press had found out where she worked and had been ringing the office to try and get her to talk to them. 'Throw them a crumb and they'll knead it into a whole loaf. If

you say nothing it will blow over within a week.'
He apologised again before ringing off.

A couple of hours later a large bunch of red
roses was delivered to the office as added conso-
lation from Leonidas, much to the excitement of
everyone at Kendon Interiors—particularly the female contingent, who had already seen the article
and were still drooling over the hard and exciting
image of the high-powered tycoon.

As arranged, he picked Kayla up himself from
the office that evening, using his car's superior
power to roar out of the business park before one
lurking newspaperman and a couple of young
girls from the office who had rushed out to get a
glimpse of him knew what had happened.

'Thank you.' Kayla looked gratefully across at
him as he brought the powerful car into the early
rush-hour traffic. 'For getting me out of there so
fast—and for the roses.' Remembering her telephone call to him earlier, however, and the manner in which she had finally got to speak to him,
she asked, before she could stop herself, 'Did you
get your secretary to send them for you?'

Wasn't that what company men did? she reflected bitterly, remembering other roses. Before

turning their focus on their adoring secretaries themselves?

'I'm not your father, Kayla,' he answered grimly, without taking his eyes off the rear window of the car in front of them, uncannily reading her mind. 'Nor am I your ex-fiancé. When I send flowers I never do it without choosing exactly what I want myself.'

Which put her in her place, good and proper! She didn't doubt that in this instance at least he was telling her the truth.

He was due to fly to the Channel Islands for a conference that weekend. Expressing concern, however, at Kayla being left to the mercies of the press for a couple of days, he instructed her not to stray beyond the boundaries of his home, and made sure she complied by instructing one strong-armed member of his security staff to keep his eye on her.

'What are you imagining I'll do if I go out?' she quipped as he was leaving for the helicopter that was standing, its blades whirring, on the landing pad in front of the house. 'Find some man to impregnate me so I can tell everybody it's yours?'

She regretted it almost as soon as she'd said it.

'You aren't a prisoner, Kayla,' he said, all emotion veiled by the dark fringes of his lashes. 'I'm only thinking of your privacy and your safety.'

And he was gone, leaving her with only the briefest touch of his lips branding her cheek.

As it was a good weekend she swam in the pool and sunbathed on the terrace, catching up with some reading and watching a couple of adventure movies in the mansion's impressive professionally equipped cinema room.

Nothing, though, could compare to her traitorous excitement at hearing Leonidas's helicopter returning on Sunday evening after she had gone to bed—deliberately early so that she wouldn't have to see him. Wouldn't have to battle with this underlying sexual tension that was building in her daily with a terrifying intensity, and which was becoming almost impossible to keep from him whenever he touched her—however casually. And she *had* to keep it from him, she thought, harrowed and racked with frustration. Because wasn't this part of his ploy? To wear her down with wanting him? Just to redeem his indomitable masculine pride? And if she did ever succumb again to her own foolish and weak-willed desire for him, what then?

No, she had to be strong, she determined. Had to resist him at all costs. Just until that contract was signed.

When Leonidas picked her up from the office the following evening it was to take her for an early dinner in a favoured bistro he knew and then, much to her surprise, on to a photography exhibition.

'I thought as you're so attached to that camera of yours,' he said, pulling up outside the small but well-attended little gallery, 'you might appreci-ate seeing what the professionals have to offer. Of course if you'd rather not...'

'No. No I'd like to,' Kayla put in quickly when he looked in two minds about whether to park or drive away. Craig had hated anything like this, and even Josh and Lorna couldn't understand what Craig had used to call her 'camera fetish'. Just the chance to be among like-minded people for a change was something she didn't want to pass up.

The exhibition, by private invitation only, was being hosted by an acquaintance of Leonidas's, and Kayla could tell as soon as they were inside that he and the gentle grey-haired man were true friends. There was none of the deference or play-ing up to Leonidas that she had seen among some of the people at the functions she'd attended with him, until she'd wondered how he could ever tell who was really sincere.

'Leonidas tells me that you're quite the enthusiast,' the man said to her, smiling. Leonidas—still dressed, as she was, in a dark business suit—was, with the rest of the twenty or so guests, browsing some of the artwork around the gallery. 'If ever you feel you have something to offer, then you know where to come.'

'It's just a hobby!' Kayla laughed warmly, wondering what Leonidas had been saying to his friend about her. That he had said anything at all gave her a decidedly warm feeling inside.

'So what do you think?' Suddenly he was there beside her, sharing her interest in a waterfall scene with some interesting use of light.

'It's good,' she expressed, enervated by his dark executive image. 'But if it had been mine I'd have toned the light down a little.' She was finding it hard to concentrate when she could feel the power of his virility emanating from him, and her nostrils were straining for every greedy breath of his cologne. 'It isn't subtle enough for me.'

'And you like subtlety?'

Dry-mouthed, Kayla touched her tongue to her

top lip and saw the way his eyes followed the nervous little action. 'Every time.' She even managed to smile, but her lips felt stretched and burning.

'Perhaps this will be more to your taste.' They had moved on and he was referring to a landscape captured beneath an angry sky.

'Much too wild,' she dismissed laughingly, and saw the sexy elevation of a dark eyebrow.

'Are you saying you prefer something more… tamed?'

There was sensuality in the way he said it, in that momentary hesitation. Or was she imagining it? she wondered, her heart still racing when he immediately invited her opinion on the technicalities of the photograph—its depth of field, how it captured the eye.

He knew a lot about the subject, and she was impressed.

'I've studied a bit,' he said modestly, when she told him so. 'Unlike you. You're a natural,' he commented, making her glow inside. 'So, what about this one?'

'Too much Photoshop,' she quipped, wrinkling her nose, and he laughed.

For a moment it felt as it had that day he had taken her to that little island and she'd been insisting on racehorses on a piece of land not a mile wide. Indulging in make-believe. Playing games with him. Except that it was different tonight. Tonight the very air around them was pulsating with a dangerous chemistry, and she wasn't with Leon, the man she'd believed to be open and carefree with scarcely two pennies to his name. She was with Leonidas Vassalio, hardened billionaire, powerful magnate and the man who had hurt her—was still hurting her just by being the type of man he was. The type who would use her concern for her friends to get what he wanted.

'My Gran used to say that the camera doesn't lie. But it does,' she accepted, suddenly feeling low-spirited. 'Maybe not in her day,' she went on, 'but in this day and age the emphasis seems to be on how much you can artificially enhance or embellish, and on what you put in or take out. You can't really tell what's real any more and what isn't. There's so much that isn't as it seems.' *Including you,* she thought achingly, and had to glance away, pretending to be temporarily distracted by the other guests milling around them so that he wouldn't see the emotion scoring her face.

'And that means so much to you?'

'Yes, it does,' she said. 'I like the camera to capture things as they really are.' She turned back to him now, her feelings brought under control. 'Men and women. Places. Things. I like them portrayed "warts and all", as the saying goes. I'm not a fan of illusion. Being fooled into seeing something that isn't really there.'

He tilted his head, the movement so slight that she wasn't sure whether she had imagined it or not. His eyes were dark pools of inscrutable emotion and she wondered what he was thinking. That he had done just that with her when he hadn't told her who he was?

'Let's go home,' he said.

He spoke very little to her on the relatively short journey back, while the car ate up the miles in the gathering dusk.

There had been a sporadic press presence at the main gates of the house over the past few days, and Leonidas wasn't taking any chances when they arrived home.

'We'll take the east entrance,' he told Kayla as he turned the car down a quiet lane that stretched for a couple of miles and which, from the manicured trees above the high wall that soon came into view, obviously skirted his property.

Another pair of electronically opened gates

brought them past a small lodge and into his home through a smaller and more secluded side entrance.

'Why isn't this part of the house used?' Kayla whispered as they came out of rooms covered in dustsheets which Leonidas had had to unlock to allow them into the main body of the house. She felt like a child creeping around when she should have been in bed. Or a guilty mistress sneaking away from the ecstasies of her lover's bed…

'I had this part converted for my father, but he never came here,' he said, his voice taking on a curiously jagged edge.

'Why not?' Kayla asked, thinking how thick and black his hair was as he stopped to lock the door behind him. It made her want to rake her fingers through it, twist the strong tufts around them as she lay beneath him, crying out from the terrifying pleasure he was withholding from her.

'I believe I told you before. We were never able to get on. I wanted us to try and establish some sort of rapport as he was getting older.' They were moving along a softly lit carpeted passage now. 'To try and forge some sort of bond with him.'

He was so close behind her that if she stopped he would collide with her, Kayla thought hectically, craving the feel of his warmth through her prim little jacket and tight pencil skirt.

'And did you?'

'No. There was too much between us—far too much to even imagine we could repair it. He didn't want to share in my good fortune or the things I could give him. He didn't want anything from me,' he concluded, with something in his voice that she might have mistaken for pain if she hadn't known better.

'Why not? Wasn't he proud of you?' she queried, feeling for him in spite of herself as they came through an archway into the main hall alongside the sweeping staircase. She couldn't believe that any parent with a son like Leonidas—driven, enterprising, so overwhelmingly successful—could possibly be anything else.

'Oh, I think he was satisfied that I'd turned out to be the man he had been determined to mould me into,' he accepted harshly.

Kayla glanced back over her shoulder and saw the rigidity of his features, the hard cynicism touching his mouth. 'And what type is that?'

'The type who understands that sentiment and idealism are for fools and that common sense and practicality are the only two reliable bedfellows.'

'Do you really believe that?' she murmured, with wounded incredulity in her eyes as she stopped, as he had, at the foot of the stairs.

'What does it matter what I believe?' he said.

He meant to her. And yet it did matter, she realised—far too much—and she had to sink her nails into her clenched palms to keep herself from blurting it out.

He was hard and ruthless. She'd realised that even before she'd left Greece. Although she hadn't known how hard and how calculating he could be until she'd seen him in full corporate action, which was how he had managed to climb to the very top of the executive ladder while still only thirty-one. Yet there was an altruistic side to his nature too, reined in beneath that cold and ruthless streak, which could have had her eating out of his hand if she had been weak enough to let it. But she wasn't, she thought turbulently as she found herself battling against a surge of responses to that dark and raw sensuality that transcended everything else about him.

'Thank you for taking me to the exhibition,' she said, in a husky voice that didn't sound like hers. 'It was thoughtful of you. I think I'll go straight up. Goodnight.'

If she had thought he would let her go then she had been fooling herself, she realised too late, when his firm, determined fingers closed around her wrist.

'You might not like the man you think I am—or what I stand for—but it excites you, Kayla.'

How right he was! She felt panicked as he drew her towards him and brought the fingers of his other hand to play along the pulsing sensitivity of her throat.

'*This* excites you.'

'No, don't—please...' It was a hopeless little sound. The sound of one who knew her cause was lost.

'Why? Are you afraid that if for one minute you let your guard down you might just have to acknowledge how much you want me?'

'I don't want you.' Rebellion warred with the dark desire in her eyes. Futile rebellion, she realised when she saw him smile.

'No?'

He was barely touching her, yet every feminine cell was screaming out to the steel-hard strength and warmth and power he exuded. She could feel her breasts straining against her blouse, could feel the moist heat of her desire against the flimsy film of her string.

'You want me and it's driving you mad. It's driving us both mad,' he admitted, and his scent and his nearness and that iron control were electrifying as he tilted her chin with a forefinger—all that was touching her now. 'You want me,' he said huskily, his dark eyes raking over her upturned mouth. 'Say it.'

It was a soft command, breathed against her lips, and it was that excruciating denial of the kiss she was craving, which finally broke her resolve.

'I want you! I want you! I want—!'

His mouth over hers silenced her wild admission in the same moment that she twined her arms around his neck to pull him down to her.

He caught her to him, those strong arms tightening around her.

Kayla wriggled against him, seeking even closer contact with his body, her own a mass of desperate wanting as their mouths fused, broke contact, devoured in a hunger of frenzied need.

He was tugging off her jacket, letting it lie where it fell, ripping buttons in his urgency to get her out of her clothes. But when her hands slid under his jacket and it fell away from those broad shoulders he suddenly swept her up off her feet and mounted the stairs with her as effortlessly as if she were a rag doll.

Of course. The staff.

The thought penetrated her consciousness, but only for a second, because all that mattered was that she was with this man, destined for his bed, and she was going to know the full meaning of his loving her.

In the physical sense...

She shook that thought away, because all she wanted was to have him inside her—anyhow, anywhere and any way it came.

He set her down on her feet before they had even reached his room, pressing her against the wall of the carpeted landing, as hungry for her mouth as she was for the pleasuring mastery of his hands on her body.

He surfaced only to tug off her gaping blouse, pulling her against his hard hips so that he could deal with the back zipper of her skirt.

It slipped to the floor and she was standing there in nothing but a white lacy bra and string and black high-heeled sandals, revelling in his groan of satisfaction as he caught her to him again.

His tongue burned an urgent trail along the shallow valley between her breasts and, clutching his shoulders, she arched against him as his mouth moved ravishingly over a lacy cup.

The fine silk of his shirt was a sensual turn-on under her urgently groping hands, the fabric of his immaculately pressed trousers heightening her pleasure as he suddenly cupped her buttocks and lifted her up and her legs went around him, her fingers tangling wildly in his thick black hair.

It was the culmination of everything he had promised and everything she had dared to imagine, she realised as they finally made it to his room and he dropped her down onto the yielding sensuality of his big bed.

They had been lovers in the spring, but it hadn't been like this, she thought as he came down to her, still fully clothed, and removed the last scraps of her underwear with swift and amazing dexterity. Perhaps he had been right when he'd suggested that his power and influence excited her. Perhaps she was no different from all those other women she'd seen visually devouring him, she thought. Because she had no control over the desires he aroused in her.

Naked, she writhed beneath him, wanting him naked too, wanting the hands that were reclaiming her body never to stop—because she had been made for them. For this…

When he moved away to hastily shed his clothes, she watched with her hair spread like wild silk over the darker sheen of his pillow, her arms arched above her head in wanton abandon to the thrilling anticipation of what was to come.

'I called you an angel once,' he said hoarsely, looking down at her from where he was standing, unashamed and magnificent in his glorious nakedness. 'But I was wrong. You're a she-devil.' It was said with a curious tremor in his voice.

'And you…' she whispered, her body pulsing as he finished sheathing himself—not taking any chances this time—and came back to join her '…are the devil incarnate.'

'Yes,' he murmured, his voice humorously soft against her lips.

But she didn't care, because she was on fire for him, burning up in a conflagration of need and wanting and desire.

Skilfully and with controlled deliberation he slid down her body, anointing her skin with kisses, although his body was taut with his own need and his breathing was as ragged as hers.

Their hunger was too demanding for much foreplay. As he moved above her, positioning himself to take her, Kayla welcomed his hard invasion, her legs opening for him like silken wings for the sun.

His sliding into her was an ecstasy she couldn't have imagined and she lifted her hips to accommodate him, a small cry spilling from her lips.

His penetration was deep, with each successive thrust taking him deeper, until he was filling her, stretching her, turning her into a being of mindless, unparalleled sensation where nothing else mattered but the union of their two bodies.

She was riding with him, being taken to a place where only the two of them existed—a rapturous world of feeling and sharpening senses that grew into a mountain of exquisitely unbearable pleasure, urging her upwards to its summit. And suddenly as she reached the top the mountain started to explode, and she cried out from the pleasure that was bursting all around her. She was falling, tumbling in a freefall of interminable sensation, clinging to the man she never wanted to let out of her arms, part of him, belonging to him, as he tumbled with her through the sensational universe.

When she came back to earth she was sobbing uncontrollably, all her pent-up feelings for him released by the shattering throbs of her orgasm.

Some time afterwards, when her sobs had sub-
sided, Leonidas asked, 'Are you all right?'

She was lying in the crook of his arm and the
warm velvet of his chest was damp from her tears.

'Yes, I'm fine,' Kayla murmured, and rolled
away from him, unable to tell him why she had
wept. If she did, then he would know, and she
didn't want to admit it to herself. So she stayed
where she was, on her side, with her legs drawn
up, not wanting to face the truth or the reality of
what had just happened.

Leonidas woke shortly before dawn.

Kayla was still lying with her back to him, as
far over on her side of the bed as it was possible
to get. With a crease between his eyes, Leonidas
slipped quietly out of bed, so as not to disturb her,
and went to take a shower.

When he returned, wearing a dark robe, she was
still sleeping, but now lying on her back. What
little make-up she'd been wearing last night was
smudged—either from his over-zealous treatment
of her or from crying, he remembered uneasily—
and her hair was alluringly tousled from making
love.

Unable to help himself, he stooped to press his

lips lightly to her forehead. She stirred slightly, her brow furrowing as though her dreams were troubled.

'Leon...'

He wasn't sure, from her soft murmur, whether that was what she'd said, but if it was it wasn't meant for the man who had made love to her last night. Not Leonidas Vassalio, corporate chairman and billionaire. Not after the way she had cried after they had made love.

She didn't trust him or even like him, and she despised herself for wanting him. Why else would she have shed tears of such bitter regret when she'd been overtaken—as he had—by their mutual passion last night?

It was his fault for thinking in the beginning that he could have a casual fling with a girl like her and that keeping the truth from her wouldn't matter. Nor had he been right in thinking he could bend her to his will in making her come here to try and get her to want him as she had in Greece. She was never likely to. She was hurting, and he had never intended that.

What was that old adage? he pondered distract-edly, moving away from the bed. If you loved something, you had to let it go. If it came back to you, it was yours. If it didn't, it never would be.

But what he felt for this beautiful, bewitching girl wasn't *love,* he thought, steeling himself against any emotion. Not as she deserved it. And she certainly wasn't his. So wasn't it time to let her go?

Wearing a silver-grey suit, white shirt and silver tie, Leonidas was perched on one of the high stools, browsing through a newspaper, when Kayla came into the huge, sterile-looking kitchen an hour or so later. Behind him the sky was overcast beyond the panoramic window, and even a myriad lights in the halogen-studded ceiling couldn't detract from the dreariness of what should have been a bright summer day.

'Good morning.' He scarcely glanced up from whatever he was reading in the *Financial Times,* although just that briefest glance from him set her insides aflame as she thought about how intimately and passionately he had pleasured her last night.

After a moment he cast the newspaper aside on the kitchen counter beside him. 'Kayla, we have to talk,' he stated without any preamble, angling his long, lean body to face her on the stool.

'About what?' she queried, with sudden queasiness in her stomach. What was he going to say that lent such a serious tone to his voice?

'I've been a moron,' he told her. 'If that's the correct expression. You were right. I have been trying to keep you in my life for the sake of my own pride—my ego, if you like—because I didn't like my ethics being brought into question in anyone's mind. Particularly the mind of a girl who was very sweet and trusting and whom I treated very unfairly when I was with her in Greece and I needed to put that right.'

'What are you saying?' Kayla queried in a small, broken voice.

'That I've been very selfish and inconsiderate and that you don't need to pander to my fragile ego any longer. Your friends' contract is assured, if that's what you've been worrying about, so you're free to cast me off…if that's what you wish,' he added with some hesitancy, and as though he was picking his words very carefully. 'Whenever you like.'

If it was what she wished?

Pain speared through her so acutely it felt like a knife slicing through the life-force of her very being. She'd never been let down and effectively rejected in such a considerately phrased manner before. But he'd got what he wanted, she thought wretchedly, trying to concentrate on her breathing. It was her total capitulation that he had needed to redeem his pride, and now she had given him that he needed nothing more.

He was just like all the others—right out of the same mould. The type of man she'd vowed never to be attracted to again. Except that this man was different. This man wasn't even capable of feeling. Not love, she accepted, anguished. He'd practically admitted that to her himself last night. Loving was a weakness—something only fools entertained— and Leonidas Vassalio was anything but weak, and certainly no fool.

'Well…' Her smile felt stretched as she tried to put on a brave face, and she wondered if she was visibly shaking as much as she was trembling inside. It occurred to her then why he'd wanted her kept out of the way of the press while he'd been away last weekend. Because he didn't want anyone thinking she was a permanent fixture in his life. 'I'd better go and start packing,' she said as tonelessly as she was able, and wondered at the unfathomable emotion that turned his eyes almost inky black.

'I have to fly to Athens,' he informed her, consulting his watch, his tone similarly flat.

It was a trip, she'd discovered, which he took on a regular basis, often going back and forth between London and his Greek office. 'If you're keen to go today, I obviously won't try and stop you, but I shan't be able to take you myself. I can, however, arrange for a car to be put at your disposal whenever you wish to leave.'

'That won't be necessary,' Kayla murmured, wanting to get out of there—and quickly—before the tears that were burning the backs of her eyes overflowed and gave her away.

He nodded as though he understood, and somehow she managed to drag herself from the room with her pride intact, safe in the knowledge that he would never know the truth. A truth she only admitted to herself now, as she stumbled over the stairs up which he had carried her so purposefully last night. That she was deeply and hopelessly in love with Leonidas Vassalio.

CHAPTER ELEVEN

MOVING LEADENLY THROUGH the silent cottage, Leonidas was checking each familiar room. He had promised Philomena's daughter he would do that for her, and that he would take anything he wanted. Anything that meant something to him, she had said.

Coming back through the kitchen, he let his glance touch painfully on a cherished oil-lamp, some sprigs of dried herbs, the stack of unused logs beside the huge stove, and his nostrils dilated from a host of evocative scents—rosemary, sage and pinewood, trapped there by shutters which remained reverently closed against the intrusion of the outside world.

There was nothing for him here. He had everything he wanted in the memory of Philomena's presence, her warmth and her voice, often scolding but always wise, and he wished fervently that she was there now, with her affectionate scolding and her wisdom.

He could hear her still, when he had run down here on countless occasions to escape his father's bellowing and his character-moulding brutality.

Be true to yourself, Leon.

But he hadn't been, had he? Not in his hopes and aspirations. In everything he hadn't been able to feel. Not since he'd been a child, or maybe a young adolescent, but certainly not as a man.

Since his mother had died and his father had blamed him for it he had built a hard, impervious shell around himself. A shell that no one, not even he himself, could crack. Only once had he ever—

He slammed the brakes on his errant thinking.

No, he hadn't been true to himself, he realised grimly. But that, like everything about this house, was now part of the past.

Grabbing one final look around filled him with such an ache of grief in his chest that he had to take a minute to steel himself before stepping outside into the bright sunlight and closing the door for the last time.

'I was just going to ring you,' Kayla said brightly as Lorna came through on her cell phone. 'The men have done a great job! The builder's been paid—in fact he's only just left—and the villa looks as good as new!'

She was standing looking up at the rafters above the galleried landing, and at the freshly rendered walls, which now bore no sign of the damage they had sustained earlier in the year. She tried not to think about how Leonidas—or Leon, she amended painfully—had rescued her that night, risking his own life in coming down here and carrying her out to the truck. She wasn't going to think about that. Or anything else about him, she decided achingly, just as she had promised herself she wouldn't when she had stepped off the ferry the previous day.

Josh hadn't been able to leave the business, and as his in-laws were away on an anniversary cruise Lorna had been fully intending to come here and do the inspection herself. But that had been before her doctor had strongly advised that she was in no condition to travel, so Kayla had immediately allayed her friend's anxieties by offering to come instead.

What she hadn't anticipated was how unbearably being here would affect her. She had known it would be painful, but just how excruciating she hadn't been prepared for. All she wanted to do now was lock up the villa, drive down and see Philomena, and then get the hell off this island before the last ferry left that day.

Now, to try and take her mind off the memories that were killing her, in a voice thickened by emotion she asked, 'Is there any news yet on that contract?'

The business that Havens Exclusive were giving them had all been agreed in principle, but the company seemed to be dragging its heels, and the paperwork that would secure it still hadn't come through. Josh and Lorna were on a knife-edge, waiting for the contract to arrive, and Kayla was secretly worried that it never would.

'That's why I'm ringing.'

The anxious note in Lorna's voice told Kayla that it still hadn't arrived.

'I rang Havens yesterday, and they seemed to think it was sent to us two weeks ago. Then today someone else said they didn't think it had been. I tried to ring Leonidas, to see if he knew anything about it, but his office said he was in Greece this week. I know you're not seeing him any more, but as you're already in the country, and as you said things between you only sort of…fizzled out…'

It had been the only way Kayla could describe her break-up with Leonidas to her friend without falling apart emotionally. 'I was wondering…is there anything you can do to get hold of him from your end? To see if you can find out what's happening?'

Lorna sounded in such a state that, although her nerves were already stretched to breaking point at the thought of calling him, Kayla agreed to help.

She knew he made regular trips between the UK and Greece, and with her heart thumping a few minutes later she got through to his Athens office.

'I'm afraid Mr Vassalio isn't here this week,' a thickly accented female voice informed her in nonetheless perfect English. 'You should be able to contact him on his mobile.'

'Thanks,' Kayla said, feeling deflated after it had taken so much courage to call in the first place.

It seemed too personal, ringing his cell phone number. Far, far too intimate… After a few moments, though, for Lorna's sake, she forced herself to do it.

'You have reached the voicemail of Leonidas Vassalio…'

Just hearing his deep tones sent fire tingling through her veins, but with her heart beating like crazy Kayla cut them off in mid-sentence. There was no way she could leave a message without her voice shaking uncontrollably. And then he'd know, wouldn't he?

She'd try him again later, she decided, breathing deeply to steady her pulse-rate. In the meantime she would do what she'd planned to do before Lorna had rung and pop down to see Philomena.

The shutters were closed when Kayla pulled up alongside the cottage, which wasn't that surprising as the late summer sun still burned fiercely here at this time of day, she thought. Even so, the flowers outside in their pots looked neglected and wilting, and there was an ominous air of emptiness about the place.

The door leading from the yard where she had sunbathed in the May sunshine looked securely closed, which was unusual, she realised, and there was no bread baking in the old clay oven, or any spotlessly clean washing hanging on the line.

As she came around the house, looking up at the shuttered windows, a man loading a cart called to her from a little way down the lane. He tilted his head, his weathered face sympathetic, and the expressive little gesture of his hands assured Kayla of what she dreaded most.

Oh, no!

As she wandered numbly around the side one

solitary chicken ran clucking across the yard, and the sound only seemed to emphasise its screaming loneliness.

Her heart heavy with grief, Kayla got into the car, fighting back the emotion she could barely contain. But she knew she had to, because if she let it out for just a moment then she'd be swamped by it, she thought. By memories that were so much a part of this place. And Leonidas...

Her cell phone was sticking out of the bag she'd tossed onto the passenger seat, jolting her into remembering that she was supposed to try and contact him again.

Did he know? About Philomena? And then she realised that of course he would know. He would be heartbroken, she thought. In which case how could she ring him and ask him about something so trivial as a contract? She couldn't. Anyway, his office had told her that he hadn't come to Athens. And yet his London office had stated categorically that he had...

Of course!

Her gaze lifted swiftly to the hillside and the invisible ribbon of road that wound up above Lorna's villa. He would have been told about Philomena and he would have come here to be with her family. Because she was *his* family. Or the only person worth calling 'family' that Leonidas Vassalio had. In which case he would be here! Not in Athens! Here! At the farmhouse! Where else would he stay?

She didn't know if the little hatchback would stand up to the punishing drive as she tore out of the lane and took the zig-zagging road up to the familiar dirt track. She only knew she had to see him. She prayed to heaven that he would be there, and that he wouldn't send her away.

The farmhouse looked the same as she swung into the paved yard. Pale stone walls. Green peeling shutters. Its rickety terracotta roof seeming to grow out of the hillside rising sharply above it. The truck was still there too, looking as dusty and as sorry for itself as it ever had.

No one answered when she knocked at the flaking door.

Coming around the back, she noticed how baked everything looked from the hot, Ionian summer, remembering with a sharp shaft of pain how she had sat there on the terrace under that vine-covered canopy, enjoying the fish Leonidas had cooked for her the first time she had come here.

Again, there was no response to her knock, and

after several attempts to make him hear she tried the doors. They were locked, just as Philomena's had been.

Everything was the same, but nothing was, she thought achingly, peering through one of the half-open shutters. Supposing he had gone? Supposing he hadn't been here at all? She couldn't bear it if he wasn't. She didn't think she'd ever find the courage to face him again.

She could see papers lying all over the kitchen table, just as there had been on that dreadful morning when she'd seduced him so shamelessly before discovering who he really was. And there was his pinboard with his plans on, propped up against the easel.

So he was immersing himself in work. Was that how he was dealing with his grief? Carrying on regardless with that formidable strength of character? That indomitable will that was such an integral part of the man she had so desperately fallen in love with?

A sound like a twig snapping behind her had her whirling round, her pulses missing a beat and then leaping into overdrive when she saw him striding up through the overgrown garden.

'What are you doing here?' He spoke in such a

low whisper that she couldn't tell whether he welcomed seeing her, but his eyes were penetrating and his features were scored with shock.

'I came to check the villa. For the builder. I mean for Lorna.' She was waffling, but she couldn't help it. Just the sight of him, in a loose-fitting, long-sleeved white shirt tucked into black denim jeans seemed to be turning her insides to mush.

He looked like the old Leon, with his chest half-bared and that thickening shadow around his mouth and chin. But his hair—only slightly longer than when she had seen him last—was still immaculately groomed, and with that air of power that Kayla could never detach from him now he was still very much Leonidas—the billionaire. He looked leaner, though, she decided, and his eyes were heavy, and she remembered in that moment that he was in mourning.

'I—I heard about Philomena.' She made a helpless little gesture. 'Just now. I went down there. I'm so…so sorry—' Tears threatened and she broke off, unable to keep the emotion out of her voice.

He merely dipped his head in acknowledgment. Perhaps he didn't trust himself to speak, Kayla thought.

'I thought you were gone. I wasn't sure if you'd

even been here, and I wanted to see you. To tell you.' She was prattling on again, but she didn't know what else to say to him. He wasn't making it particularly easy for her.

As he crossed the flagstones, taking his key out of his trouser pocket, she was struck, as she always was, by the grace and litheness with which he moved, and by his sheer, uncompromising masculinity.

'Is that why you came?' He glanced over his shoulder as he stooped to unlock the door.

'Yes,' she answered, because it *was* the only reason. She would never have had the courage to seek him out over anything less.

'And who told you I was here?' He pushed open the door, gestured for her to go inside.

'No one. I just put two and two together,' she said, moving past him with every cell responding to the aching familiarity of him beneath her flimsy feminine tunic and leggings.

'And came up with four?' He sounded impressed as he followed her in. 'What made you so sure I was in the country?'

'I'd been trying to ring you,' she admitted, and then felt like biting off her tongue. But the atmosphere of the ancient farmhouse, with its familiar rusticity and evocative scents, was so overwhelming that she hadn't stopped to think.

'Oh?' His tone demanded more as he guided her into the sitting room. It looked the same, with its jaded walls and tapestries and its faded striped throws over the easy chairs. 'What about?' He gestured for her to sit down.

'Lorna's been getting worried,' she said, subsiding onto the sofa. 'I'm sorry,' she murmured, seeing the grooves already etched around his eyes and mouth deepening. 'I didn't want to mention it. Not right now.'

'The world has to keep turning,' he said, sounding resigned. 'Do you want some coffee?'

'Something cold,' she appealed, thinking that nothing seemed so cold and detached from her as he did right then. She wondered if she should have come; wondered painfully if he was annoyed with her because she had.

He returned minutes later with two tall frosted glasses of an iced citrus drink.

'So Lorna's worried?' he reminded her as she sipped the liquid gratefully. It was sharp and very refreshing. 'What about?'

'They haven't received the contract that Havens were supposed to be supplying.'

'Supposed to be?' His eyes were darkly penetrative as he set his own glass down on a side table.

'I was just worried that…'

'Yes?'

Why was he looking at her like that? Kayla wondered. As though he wanted to plunder her very soul?

'…that you might have changed your mind. About giving them that order.'

There. She had said it. So why didn't she feel any relief? And why was he looking at her with his mouth turning down in distaste, as though she was something that had just crawled out from one of the cracks in the walls outside?

'So you still think I'd do that? You are still so shot through with doubt and suspicion over what your father and your fiancé did to you that you think every man who carries a briefcase and has a secretary can't be anything but an unscrupulous bastard?'

'That's not true!'

'Isn't it?' he shot back. 'We're a type. Isn't that what you said?'

He was standing above her, hands on hips, his legs planted firmly apart. It was such a dominant pose that her gaze faltered beneath his. With heart-quickening dismay she realised she had let it fall to somewhere below his tight lean waist—which was worse.

'Well, it's true, isn't it?' she said, hurting, feeling her body's response to his hard virility even as he stood there actively judging her. 'You lied to me about everything! Every single thing! And when I didn't like it you used my friends to blackmail me into living with you until...'

'Until what?' he pressed, relentless.

'Until you'd got what you wanted.'

'And what was that?' His eyes were shielded by the thick ebony of his lashes and his question was an almost ragged demand.

'You know very well.'

'No, I don't. I'm afraid you're going to have to spell it out for me.'

'Until you'd got me to go to bed with you.' There were flags of pink across her cheekbones, lending some colour to her pale skin beneath the summer-bleached gold of her loose hair. 'Wasn't that the whole idea of having me move in with you?' she said wretchedly. 'To salvage your pride and your ego? Wasn't it enough that you made a complete fool out of me without robbing me of my dignity and my self-respect as well?'

'Is that what I did?' His eyes as they met hers held some dark, unfathomable emotion. 'I really didn't realise that in making love with me you were sacrificing all that.'

The raw note in his voice had her searching his face with painful intensity, but his features were shuttered and unreadable.

Her fingers were icy around the glass, but she couldn't seem to feel them. She couldn't feel anything except her aching love for him and the raw agony of seeing him again when he didn't share her feelings, when he had admitted to being incapable of love—virtually ridiculing it—that night he had carried her to his bed.

'I just wasn't happy being another notch on your bedpost,' she murmured, looking down at the striped fabric covering the sofa and wondering what had happened in his life to make him so hard-bitten as she plucked absently at a loose strand of the faded weave.

'Neither was I. That was why I let you go.'

'That was very magnanimous of you.' Her throat was clogged with emotion. Pray heaven that he didn't guess just how much he had hurt her!

'Just as well I did—in the circumstances,' he

said. 'I wouldn't have been able to keep my hands off you if you had stayed.'

The 'circumstances' meaning the loss of her dignity and self-respect, Kayla realised painfully, wanting to tell him that making love with him had been the most intense and pleasurable experience of her life.

'Well, you can tell Lorna that she doesn't need to worry...' Suddenly he was talking about business, dismissing what had happened between them as easily and as ruthlessly as he had dismissed her from his life. 'That contract should have been with Kendon Interiors over two weeks ago. I'll get on to Havens right away and your friends will have it within the next forty-eight hours.'

So he hadn't been withholding it, Kayla thought. She had satisfied his requirements and he was up-holding his part of the bargain. She just wished it hadn't cost her so much to make it possible. But it had. And it hurt—like hell.

'What's wrong?'

Through the crushing emotion that seemed to be weighing her down she caught his hard yet strangely husky enquiry. His eyes were narrowed, probing, digging down into her soul again, and Kayla sucked in a panicky breath as he moved closer. He'd claimed her body as his own, and she would bear the brand of his consummate lovemaking for the rest of her life, but she wasn't going to let him know that he had branded her heart as well!

'I'd better go.' She leaped up, spilling some of the juice she had scarcely touched over her clothes and over the flags. 'Oh, no...'

'I'll get you a towel.' The glass was retrieved from her shaking hand.

'I can do it myself,' she told him, her voice cracking.

'Kayla!'

There was a thread of urgency in his voice but she took no heed of it as she stumbled along to the kitchen. The pain of loving him was like a knife piercing her heart.

It would be so easy to break down. To let him see how much she cared. But if she did that then she would only be inviting more humiliation—and ultimately more pain. He would use her again, solely in the name of pleasure. And she would let him, she thought wildly, knowing she had to clean herself up as quickly as she could and get as far away from this place—from him—as was humanly possible.

She'd been a fool to come, she realised, grabbing several sheets of kitchen paper from the roll that hung next to the sink and starting to dab it hastily over her wet tunic. She should have telephoned him. E-mailed. Anything but risk coming here and putting herself through this. But she'd wanted to see him. Speak to him. What kind of a first-rate fool did that make her? She was a glutton for punishment if she'd imagined that coming here—even if it was purely to offer him her sympathies over Philomena—would leave her unaffected and unscathed. And if she'd been hoping, even subconsciously, that seeing him again might change the status quo between them, then she'd forgotten—or was choosing to ignore—every lesson she'd thought she had learned. For all his good points—and there were a lot of them—he was still a ruthless businessman. A self-confessed, hardheaded realist, who believed that love and sentimentality were for fools.

Well, she'd leave him to his laptop and his papers and his…

Plans?

The word died from her consciousness as she swung painfully round to face them, having tossed the damp, scrunched-up kitchen roll into the bin. The easel was angled towards the front window, which was why she hadn't seen it when she'd peered through the back shutters earlier. But the pinboard was a canvas, and what she'd thought were plans was...

A full-length painting of *her!*

He had captured her as she must have looked that day coming out of the sea, wearing only her white smock-top and bikini briefs. Her hair was blowing loose and she was looking down at something in the water, her golden lashes accentuated with a sensuality she had never attributed to them before. What she was wearing was sheer, yet her body was indistinct through the folds of virginal gossamer. It was a work of bold strokes. Movement. But above all else of the soul. Only a man could have painted her with such intrinsic sensuality, she thought. A man who loved his subject. Who knew her inside and out...

She put her hand up as though to touch it and as quickly retracted it, her fingers curling into a tight ball which she pressed to her mouth as tears started to fall.

They had changed to racking sobs in the time it took Leonidas to cross from the doorway and reach her.

'Kayla...' The depth of her emotion tore at him

and she put up no resistance as he pulled her into his arms.

She was crying for Philomena. He wasn't blind enough not to know that. She was remembering where she had come from that day and who she had been staying with…

'Oh, my darling beautiful girl, don't cry.'

He'd intended to say it in Greek, and only realised when she lifted her head and looked at him with soul-searching intensity that he had said it in English—and that it was too late.

'Why didn't you tell me?' she breathed in a shocked little whisper.

'About the painting?' His voice trembled with emotion as he used his thumb to wipe away her tears. 'Or about being in love with you?'

There. It was out now, he thought, and he would have to bear the consequences of baring his soul.

'What?' Kayla couldn't believe that she was hearing properly. 'About the painting…' She shook her head as though to clear it—uttered a little laugh through her tears. 'Both!' Was he really saying this? Hectically, her eyes searched his face.

'Why do you think I wanted you with me?' he uttered deeply, on a shuddering note, hardly daring to believe that she wasn't ridiculing him.

'To salvage your pride.' Pain lined her forehead as she remembered that last morning. 'You said so yourself.'

'Well, there was a bit of that, I'll admit.' He pulled a self-deprecating face. 'But mainly it was because I wanted to get you to trust me again. There was no other way I could think of that would break through the barriers you'd erected against me—and not just because I hadn't been straight with you in the beginning, but because you believed I was the type of man who had hurt you so badly before—the type you so clearly despised. I was hoping you would look beyond the outer shell and see that I was different from those other men you'd known. Yet I only compounded my mistakes by browbeating you into staying with me. I would never have gone back on my word over that contract. But when I realised that you really believed I was manipulative enough to be using your friends to get to you—was actually capable of destroying everything they had if you didn't do exactly what I wanted—I guess it was more than a crushing blow to my pride. I decided I didn't have anything to lose. I needed to earn your respect. That's why I wanted to take things slowly for a while and not complicate matters by taking you to bed, though it was torture having to exercise enough restraint not to do so. When we did make love and you cried I knew it was because your heart didn't want it, even though physically you couldn't resist this thing we have between us any more than I could.'

'That isn't true,' Kayla denied emphatically, knowing she had to tell him now. 'I was crying because I love you—because the whole experience for me had been so...so amazingly incredible. And because I knew—thought—you didn't feel anything for me and that sooner or later you'd want me to go. And you did,' she reminded him, with all the agony of the past few weeks rising up to torment her again. 'Why? If you feel the same way I do?'

'Because I didn't fully realise it—or want to acknowledge it—until after you'd gone,' he admitted, his chest lifting heavily, 'and I didn't want to hurt you any more than I knew I already had.'

'And all the time you've been doing this...' She pulled back from him slightly to gaze awestruck at the painting. 'Wow! Do I really look like that?'

'You'd better believe it,' he said, with a sexy sidelong grin.

'It's brilliant. You're a genius,' she praised, and he laughed. 'No, I'm serious,' she breathed, meaning it. She couldn't understand why, with so much talent, he hadn't made art his career.

He made a self-deprecating sound down his nostrils when she asked him. 'There were reasons,' he divulged almost brokenly.

'What reasons?' she pressed gently, realising that it was stirring up some deeply buried pain for him to talk about it.

'My father had other ideas for me,' he said. 'He wouldn't countenance having a son who painted for a living. He thought it less than manly. We argued about it—and never stopped arguing about it.' And now he had started pouring out his most agonising secret he couldn't stop. 'We were arguing about it in the car the night my mother died. If I hadn't been determined to oppose his will he wouldn't have kept turning round to shout at me and we would never have had the accident that killed her. I wouldn't let up when I knew I should have, and it was my mother who ultimately paid the price. After that even the thought of painting was abominable to me. How could it be anything else?' he suggested, his strong features ravaged by the pain he had carried all these years. 'Knowing that she'd died because of it. Because of *me!*'

'You didn't kill her!' Kayla exhaled, understanding now what devils had been driving him all his life to make him so hard-headed and single-mindedly determined—understanding a lot of things now. 'You were—what? Fourteen? Fifteen? Barely more than a child! Your father was the driver. He was also an adult. It was up to him to exercise restraint until he'd stopped the car.'

'My father didn't see it like that,' he relayed. Yet for the first time he found himself taking some solace from the tender arms that went around him, from the gentle yet determined reasoning in her words.

Art was feeling and feelings were weakness. His father had indoctrinated that into him. But the feelings he had for this beautiful woman—which were being unbelievably reciprocated—made him feel stronger than he had ever felt in his life.

'This house…it's yours, isn't it?' Kayla murmured, with her head against his shoulder. 'This is where you lived when you were a boy.'

Locked in his arms, she felt the briefest movement of his strong body as he nodded. 'It was the first time I'd been able to bring myself back here since my father died last year. The first time I'd been back—apart from visits to Philomena—in over fifteen years.'

His voice cracked as he mentioned the grandmother figure who had filled the void when he had been left motherless and without the nucleus of a loving family. Understanding, Kayla held him closer. Hadn't she lost a grandmother too?

'I love you,' she whispered. It was the only thing it felt right to say just then.

He smiled down at her and her heart missed a beat when she recognised the sultry, satisfied response of the man she had fallen in love with. 'I love you too—very much, *psihi mou*. We may not have got off to a very good start, but knowing you has made me see that there are more important things in life than everything I've been pursuing. Oh, money and position are wonderful to have, but they're nothing without the most precious things in life—like a caring partner and a family. Without love,' he murmured against her lips, acknowledging it indisputably now. 'Do you think you would find it too much of a punishment to marry a company man with a briefcase and a secretary—who, incidentally, is fifty-three years old and worth her weight in gold? A man who—also incidentally—*does* own an island and builds eyesores for a living? Though not literally. He leaves the spade and shovel work to his minions nowadays.'

He was joking about the minions. She could hear it in his voice. But she couldn't believe he was actually asking her to be his wife.

'Of course if you don't want to…' He was looking so uncertain, so vulnerable, that she reached up and brought his head down to hers.

'Leonidas Vassalio, of course I'll marry you,' she whispered smilingly, before she kissed him and felt the surge of power that trembled through his body as he caught her to him. 'Leon…'

That's better, his eyes said approvingly when he lifted his head, and the gleam in their dark depths promised everything that was joyous and exciting. 'And now…' suddenly he was sweeping her up into his arms '…I believe we have some unfinished business upstairs.'

Much later, after he'd gone to make some coffee, Kayla was surprised when he returned almost immediately.

'Your cell phone is bleeping,' he told her, handing over her bag, and she was alarmed to see the display on her phone showing half a dozen missed calls—all from Josh.

'Lorna's in hospital,' she told Leonidas when she'd finished speaking to her friend's husband.

'She was rushed in for a Caesarean section this afternoon but everything's OK.' She was laughing and crying as she added, 'Both mother and daughter are doing well!'

'Thank heaven for that!' he expressed, with his hand against his robed chest, looking as thrilled and almost as relieved as Kayla felt. 'This means we have to get a move on if we want to catch up with Josh and Lorna—particularly if you're going to fill my island with dogs and horses and babies, Mrs Vassalio. It's in the Bahamas, by the way. And at this exact moment I can't do too much to fulfil your dreams with the first two things on your wish-list, but I can certainly do something right now about fulfilling the last!'

Later, lying in his arms, Kayla stirred and stretched contentedly.

He's a good man, Philomena had tried to tell her, and Kayla knew that now. She also knew that as men came—company or otherwise—they didn't come any better.

* * * * *

Mills & Boon® Large Print

October 2013

THE SHEIKH'S PRIZE
Lynne Graham

FORGIVEN BUT NOT FORGOTTEN?
Abby Green

HIS FINAL BARGAIN
Melanie Milburne

A THRONE FOR THE TAKING
Kate Walker

DIAMOND IN THE DESERT
Susan Stephens

A GREEK ESCAPE
Elizabeth Power

PRINCESS IN THE IRON MASK
Victoria Parker

THE MAN BEHIND THE PINSTRIPES
Melissa McClone

FALLING FOR THE REBEL FALCON
Lucy Gordon

TOO CLOSE FOR COMFORT
Heidi Rice

THE FIRST CRUSH IS THE DEEPEST
Nina Harrington

0913 Rom LP